I0586985

StellarCosm
First Printed 2022

This is a work of fiction, I literally made it all up; if any of the things end up coming true
that would be super amazing, but ultimately the result of fantastic coincidence.

Typeset using:
Ubuntu
Ubuntu Condensed
Roboto Condensed
Roboto Condensed Lite
Alegreya Sans
Bergell LET
& if you look *really* carefully
Alegreya SC

Cover Illustration : Ranger Spinks
Cover Photo: Guillermo Ferla

Paperback: 978-0-6454871-0-7
Hardcover: 978-0-6454871-1-4
Ebook: 978-0-6454871-2-1

Any typographical er rors
found in th!s document
are 100% intentional.

Concrete Prose
Form ~ Style ~ Defiance

Space; is this really big place in which lots of stuff happens
~ p. Grlgenheim

C O O R D I N A T E S

1

In a neighbouring galaxy
The Voyager Space Probe *(#1)* drifts through space *bleeping* **transmitting** *keep on keepin' on* **goddamned antiquated but ignorance is bliss** it's the furthest reaching endeavor of humankind to date—a fantastically lucky bombardment of strahlend particles has kept it running all this time—rudimentary language binarises its dumb cheerful greeting 0 1 1 0 1 0 0 0 0 1 1 0 1 0 0 1 *yeah!* Several hundred th000sand lightyears of talking to no-one in particular has made the Voyager a little...   ...kooky...

                     –Tonk–
                     Oh!

It bumps indelicately into a V A S T space vessel —— Nearby **small** hatch opens in the colossal hull of the ship and an eyeball on MECHanical arm emerges and scrutinises **blinks** *whirrs* & views the strange archaic device

1010101010110001001010110111010101110101010010100101101010
11010110101010101101100101 / Hiya! / 11101011010111011101011101
0100111110101010101010101010110110010111101011010110001 11
says the Voyager

[FsagÆae§rgfa¿#ÅζÇÐđ»ξφ♯¶נ]
says the eyeball

Stellar views into Swirling fog... *it's smoke* & an extremely close cigarette butt swings into view *It is spinning about in zero-gravity* This is the ashtray of the circular bar   The centrifical force keeps planetweight around the inside rim *the polished fungwood bartop* **the ashtray is the hub...**

...just flick up

It all started with the droid...
Says Lojol; he's the one sitting beside the drunken Interjelly
Or it could have been the hooker.
Lojol is a loose looking individual **smoking** mostly male in a one-piece silk black jumpsuit *his hair is the same black silk of the suit* on closer inspection he wears a grim countenance *&nd looks worse for wearing it too* Flicks his cigarette butt upwards into the zero-g hub
...Aw stuff it, I'll start from the moment I was discovered.
Which was when he was slipping a disk into his jacket pocket
Which was descending hard on a floating village inside a giant popcorn
Which was when the voyager probe softly collides with an alien spacecraft

Hang on, where was I?

discovered discover discove **Voyager Collides Spacecraft** didiscovered discocovered discovered disco coverdisco **Floating Inside Popcorn** discoveroed discoveredddd discovered discovere iscoverd **Disk Jacket Pocket** re discove discovered overed discored verdisco verso **Moment Discovered** overdiced core discover

Ah yes, I was discovered. Discovered stealing some tech
If you recall he was pocketing the disk An observation probe **p!ps** out of the console in front of him *klaxons start to wail instantly*

The red lights start flashing everywhere

UNAUTHORIZED POSSESION!

Says the probe

Lojol stares at it for a brief moment ***infusing a heady mix*** of adrenalines from subordinate glands before punching it — *violently* — It limply topples on its segmented arm ***plop*** & he promptly flees

flies

flits

frits

=FRITZ=

goes the probe

I'm pretty honest for a guy who pinches things for a living.
Running down a corridor guards appear behind **and then ahead** firing their
singlehand Goopguns *adheres one of the opposite guards to the wall*
So our protagonist dives **headfirst**
down a chute in the wall

I mean, the people that employ me, they're the crims. I just steal stuff.
He slides ***up?*** out the other end of the chute through the hole in the floor of a
round corridor *there is no gravity here* and glides **extremely fisheyed** through
the multiform cCTV screens of the SpacePlaceSec office
Lojol heads for a grille on the other side of the round corridor **rips it off**
squeezes down a very hexatight tunnel *shoulders crunched* **scraping**
and into a corridor identical to the one before
A small droid is floating there *minding it's own business* Lojol punches it
fatally into the wall and steals its smouldering cigarette   ***big drag!***

It's a legitimate job, you know.
Well, it's a living at any rate.
He emerges through another vent into a busy area & dives **breaststroking**
downwards ———————————————— Seats himself at the bar
ordering a drink with a flick of his wrist
The bartender droid with a famous face projected two "nches from its surface
nods   &   the   hovering   face   winks   its   glit*chyge*neric   wink
Lojol pulls a small portable monitor from his belt **props it on the bartop**
A female face pixelates onto the screen

[Don't beat yourself up about it Lojol]
[I appreciate this, what you're doing for me]
Says Janet

You bet your sweet derrière, babe!
Lojol replies *she's his digitised girlfriend* he strokes **and lusts** at the screen

[Keep your head down; Security] **Says Janet** *[Let me fix your hair]*
Lojol's hair promptly changes colour and he takes an innocent gulp of his
drink—several guards stalk along behind him **scrutinising the crowds**
They move on

The sell for this job is easy, I'm actually meeting him here.
He checks casually to see where the guards have gone
[All clear. Who are we meeting here?]
An old friend of mine. Frank.

Frank is part of the collective association known as **Ubor**
They're a freaky bunch *into immortality through BioNics* that sort of thing
Not the sort to trifle **or associate** with ———————— *but Frank is mostly harmless*
He just happened to be in the system.
Was planning to hire some local freebooter but...
...found out Lojol was here
He'd like Janet to think Frank insisted on his services because *He's the kind*
of guy that gets things done but really it's because Frank knew he'd do it as
a favour *if you know what I mean.*
Let's just say Lojol owes him one

Oop, time for business my dear.
Finishes his drink in a gulp ——————— **clips** *the monitor* **to his belt** and heads off
Enters   a   darkened   corner   *semi   secluded*   with   a   curtain
Inside two brightly coloured eyes glimmer
Frank, how's it goin' me old—
Did you get it?   **Interrupts** Frank
voice modulates under the strain of his nerves
Whoa! Pleased to meet you too, pal, long time no see.
Nice peepers by the way, they new?

Frank **sits eager** his eyes *strobe rainbow colours* make little whirring noises

You got it didn't you? When? Tell me!
Lojol checks his watch

'Bout ten minutes ago.
Frank is ecstatic *he can hardly control himself from giggling* **one of his eyes begins to twitch fiercely** pulling his cheek muscle ridiculously high

You alright Frank?
Frank becomes very defensive & serious **but the eye keeps twitching** It starts to ooze thick fluid

Yes. Give me the file.
Lojol hands him the disk *Franks defective eye squirts more ocular fluid* The vacuum pores on that cheek **and around his brow** dilate and start to hum The goo is absorbed as quickly as it seeps out

Y'know, you really should have that looked at.

Ooze squirt *o o z e*

What?

Squirt *s q u i r t* **hoov**

Oh...   ...nuthin'
Frank types *a meagre* payment into a Scanr and Lojol wipes wrist across it ʙʟ!ᴘ

As he walks out past the curtain and through the bar he whispers to Janet
I sure hope you copied that file, Janet.
[You bet I did, lover boy]
Great. Cos that's what's paying for your bod, darlin'.

Has just descended from MegaSpace, and is getting attacked by a bunch of wasp*like inspired* spacecraft **this is her chance** the whole ship is under attack ALARM! *AL!RT!* people are running everywhere She pulls on her bootlocks *grabs her hand computer* and joins them

One half of the corn cob breaks apart delicately **shedding the fighter kernels** *By contrast* the escape kernels that receive too much damage just blast straight off at full speed She is in one of the last rings to leave *but still jumps down into the cockpit from a run at the last moment*

And we're off! As the twenty *or so* craft disengage from the primary engine cob.
/SQUADRING/FIFTEEN/ /COME/IN/
/GLAD/TO/SEE/YOU/MADE/IT/SEVENTEEN/
Yeah yeah, spare me.
As she climbs into her harness **she looks just like Janet!** the kernel rotates automatically to face the target ——————— it is still being run by the Cob
/ENGAGE/TENTACLES/
/YOU/SEE/'EM/FOLKS/ /GO/GET/'EM!/
And the last wave of attack kernels take off towards the melee

The *long strands of* assault tentacles float eerily in front of them **arcing** with electric menace   Varta **that's her name** lags though and disempowers the @tactors

She recalls a program from her hand computer—on the screen the image and statistics of an enemy Insectcraft appear

Part of the console in front of her ***the Geliface*** is a large globe with a hole filled with ooze for her hand ——————————————————— instead she shoves in as much as she can of the HandComp **InterGel seeps into the socket & data leaks out** forcing the tentacles to extend as one solid bar out front *arcing with cORRuPtEd software*

The hubbub of battle communications *from the intercom* babble mutely as she steers her fighter towards a bright blue dot in the distance **decidedly away from the action** when extra loud over the squad channel —— *squAWK!*

/WHERE/THE/HELL/ARE/YOU/SEVENTEEN/?/

She puts her hand up to the globe   feigning flight position

Just chasin' a bogey cap'n. I'm right on his tail, see?

/AHH/YES/I/SEE/—/KEEP/AT/IT//DON'T/LET/HIM/LURE/YOU/TOO/FAR/

Willdo ————— ASIDE ————— *Moron.*

Varta reaches to the viewer and flicks it off with content

Sits back in her harness **hands behind her head and** feet up on the console

The fighter kernel blasts *at full speed* towards the planet

VartaLobelia, EX-fighter Seventeen, you have just successfully defected.

THE KELP FARMER VILLAGE...

On a smallish planet **blue** *mostly due to* the atmosphere and approximately 87% of the surface being covered with H2O a *medium sized* kelp farm undulates on the mild surface of a vast ocean

In the sky above *silent* pops and flashes in an area of the sky indicate an offworld battle the farmers know little of **nor do they care** The smaller nodes of domiciles linked in fringes around the primary communal node *with knuckled rods* are in turn linked together with more rods like *a spiders web* or ***an algal bloom*** The farmers tend the fields suspended between the web of infrastructure under the blazing sun

A good day...
Greets one to another **referring to** the weather – the harvest
the honest toil
Ya. the rural life
replies the other
They are simple folk *hypocrites* both embracing and eschewing technological advance

Not much motion of late.
He gazes **slightly concerned** at the calm horizon
Ya...
Three fields over **other farmers** *are talking* one pointing up at the pyrotechnics
The first two farmers look up also in the sky
It's been seen before.
Ja.

One of the flares *of the offworld skirmish* breaks the surface of the atmosphere **heats up** bursts into flames ***slowly g r o w s closer***

Oh...
...shouldn't hit us...
Close tho'...
Ya.

One of the distant farmers dives into the water between the kelpnets
Someone should tell Darg...

The farmer dives deeper **he is fit** *strong* cool waters wash kelp sweat as he swims to the UnderLock of the primary node

Secondary breathing *gills* mean
genetic engineering
he is calm in
his desc
ent

. . .

. .

.

Kelp farmer climbs around the lip of the UnterFontäne **entrance** to the village dome **gravity is confused at this moment** breaks the water's surface inside and ascends a stairway *to the Obs/Com bubble*

Have you seen it?
Yes. Don't worry, it'll splash about a klik from here.
The motion'll be good.
Taps a gauge which reads PRIMARY Ω the needle **points to** just above EMPTY

Shall I ring the house siren?
Another screen displays *the wireframe image of* a CornCob fighter column graph figures show various statistics **going into the red** *Nein. Prepare a craft, there might be a survivor…*
…or hardware.

At the fringe of the community *two farmers make ready* a 30ft boat with a curious pro**puls**ion system

2

1110101010100101101010101011011001011100101010101010101010

1011010111010111010101 / Hey / 11001 / ah... / 1001011010101010101010

10101010100101 / I'm not really supposed to stop voyaging / 001010100100100

1010101101110101101 / 'Cos y'know... I'm Voyager / 101010101010010101001

00010101010010101010110101010101011010010010100110101100

110111000110111010110111101 / Hello? / 010010101010110010110 0110

101101101011100101 / um... is there anybody here? / 0110001011010100110

11010101100110010110010101 0 / I mean... / 100110110111101010101001

10100101011001110 / I'm *all for* meeting new folks / 100101010101101110 0

011001010111001010100 / seeing new things / 1010111100001110010110

011101010110010101010010101001010101010110010101010010101

00101001111001 10 / I *am* sort of an ambassador you know / 10100101001100100

1101001101100110110101 / It's kinda my job / 01011010110110100110011

010011001001101011010 1 / my role in life / 1101000110110101000101 0

110010011010101011011010 / my Raison d'etra / 0101101010101010101100110

101010000110100 / haha / 100110111101 001 / as it were / 1000110101010101

010011010101011001010101001011011 101101010001011010110110110111 0

110101000110100110101 / You speak French? / 0110001101010101010010 10

101010101101110101001011101000110111101010011011110101 0 1

0000000000000000000000000000000000000000000000000000000000

The lights come on **unspeakably** bright
Voyager *floats* in a cavernous room
In*distinguish*able figures lurk **blobs** on the periphery of its sensors
One word is spoken

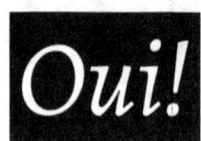

The giant corn kernel **which served as a fighter unit for the Main Cob** was a mere speck in relation to the blue planet it was heading for
It's occupant
VartaLobelia
an unwilling drone of the Collective *is defecting*
The Cob Collective are **ostensibly** mercenary traders throughout the galaxy but *really?* their primary workforce and income have evolved from *a sordid history of* —————————— press-gangery and —————————— *slavery*

Of all the dumb things you've done in your life, Varta;

> Like getting married to an Interjelly
> Like selling her persona
> Like pilfering eyes

Signing up for the Cob
when you could've just done your time in stasis
was probably the dumbest.

...except **perhaps** defecting before her time was up

The fighter kernel **shudders** heats up *bursts into flames* the blue planet looms

HUGE

closer

Jehooz!

Warnings: *Bleepers!* SIRENS! Flashflashflash!

C'mon...

Opens the SwitchGuard labeled RE-ENTRY JACKET *Click!*

N o t h i n g happens

Click!up Click!down Click!up

FLICKUp!DownUpDownUp!

The kernel glows red hot

WHITE HOT

blue at the edges! **Heat***ping!*

The kernel casing is *transformed* popcorn exterior

Descent is slowed **but** splashdown is hard

Bobbing *ultrabuoyance* on a mild sea

A 30ft boat **with curious pro***pul***sion** advances

Y'know, I could just pinch one for you...
Lojol lusts over an **eight foot** Nubian/Heechee hybrid
[Don't you dare]
I meant on the bum!
The NubiHeech winks **a sales reflex** enticement   *The window models are*
given just enough AI to sell themselves **not enough to actually think**
[You're a pig, you know that?]
And a tease. Oink oink.
[Honestly, I don't know why I put up with you]
Which is exactly why I love ya.
Janet **on his belt** is shocked *but flattered* —— she fusses at her gingham dress
...
A Japanese geisha *model iii* starts licking her index finger **in a porno way**
muscling in on the NubiHeech's territory
[C'mon Lojol, stop tormenting these poor shells]
Uh oh! Rivalry *She's pissed off!* **in a code error kind of way**
Aw, OK. Suppose we should get to the next job.
[I've plotted our course to the Learsi system, hunnybun]
As they walk away **in the background** the two 'droidshells are wrestling each
other in **the type of** angry competition **they're programmed** that could be
mistaken **for nude mud-wrestling** *to excite and titillate passers-by*
Hmm. Is the ship ready?
[Just 18 minutes ago]

Frank scoots along on **replaced feet** wheels *looks a bit like the ancient &
immortal Pan* across a bridgeway that is neuv*old* by design **unnecessary but
part of the ideals** of the collective   Its all <u>very</u> gothic
         Creatures of **varying degrees of** mechanisation bustle about the business
                    involved in the daily upkeep *of what is essentially a cult*
He holds the stolen disk between robothumb and fingerflesh **carefully**
he is not as wealthy as most Ubor members [UNITS] and so cannot afford the
best **of the best** of the nest

                         . He enters the chambers of the founding figures
All units in the collective are equal **shh! It's capitalism! but some are more
equal than others** *yeah?*
                    Ah. Frank 14354837X has returned.
The *eldest* elder ——————— Only his brain & **part of** his spine **remain** organic
                         Very good.
A megalyth ——————— Like a man who has swallowed a metalwork shop
                    We knew he was... the one ⇐
The second eldest ——————— Humandroid for the most part *knows Franks type*
                    ⇒ *for the job.*
His better half —————— **a modest fembot** tethered *married!* with coaxial bundles
Frank is ***suckered by*** enraptured of them **will eventually be one** much to their
chagrin —— which is why they cajole him **with olde-world impress-ion**
to do the most illegal of tasks   *They hope that he will be caught*
                    Your Eminences...
                    & he feeds the disk reverently into *the receiving port of* the Eldest

The Elder flares **enraged** steam escapes **&** arclight jolts here and there

You young fool!

It has been copied.

Worthless ⇐ ⇒*unit!*

Is it useless?

beg ——————————————————————————— grovel

Yes!

The other must be found.

Who copied?!

He will try ⇐ ⇒*to sell it again.*

[Tell us!] [4]

Yes, yess. Yerrrrrrtttthhh. O-o-o-ok-k-k-kkk.

His ***aftermarket*** components fail under duress

L-l-l-l-l-l-llll-o-o-ojj-ooooooollll

snivel ——————————————————————————— scrape

We are not amused!

A skip-tracer will be sent.

Who ⇐ ⇒*copied?*

L-o—   L-Oo—   LllooOOOoo—

His head twists **disgustingly** at the neck trying to articulate ***the words*** he ends up typing it on his Hexamon display **it illuminates** from the top of his shoulder

[=LOJOL=]

grovel ——————— *I'm ssorry. Forrrgive me.* ——————— beg

The tracker will work.
Yes. We think that Frij542384M will ⇐
⇒handle things.
Frank14354837X will accompany Frij542384M.
Yes.
Yes.
Y⇐ ⇒es.

They hope that Frank will disappear by some **unfortunate** accident

It will be a redeeming gesture by Frank14354837X.
Redeeming…

—ponders Frank

Frij542384M has already been informed of the situation.
You will meet at her travelcraft ⇐ ⇒departing immediately.
Er…

…immediately?

Goodbye Frank14354837X.

Spoken with firm**ly hope**ful finality

Lojol strides in **bold as megabrassica** dwarfed by the *cavernous!* expanse of
—————————————————— MAINTENANCEZONE ——————————————————

Jumps on a plataxiform and is whisked away to one of the thousand portals
that   snake   *conduitenticles*   to   the   hundreds   of   docked   vessels
swims   *breastroke*   *again*   through   the   gellid   tube   *peristalsis!*
to the scuffed hatch of his own craft

Outside ; tinpot - rustbucket overused *only 16 owners!* pride o' the pirates?
*con*verted modified re-fused enhanced **The Lojolian**
Hmm—Ego much?

Inside ; a mess of flexible cooling pipes worming through the tight corridors
unbound He doesn't like to advertise *Good old 20thC gaffa tape*
Worth more than FRACTALLOY on the commodities market
Though he keeps a stash *in an e~crypt~ed* compartment

[Crusty neons dangle **like afterthoughts** from the unclad ceiling]

Bundles of **raw&miscoloured** wiring bulge from *missing* wall panels

Not quite the poop like ships of old *but it amuses him so* to call it that a room barely large enough to accommodate the one-man navigation tank **it's homemade & square** There is a console with a jack for his portable monitor **this is where Janet** *oversees* **lives** — The tank itself is **jury rigged** CLEERSTEEL cracked and patched in places *to stop the interface gel from leaking out* Braces of whatever was handy at the time **prop** between the walls & the tank to stop it from deteriorating further **busting open entirely!** Makes it look like a refridgerator *cross* sea urchin has taken residence
Space makes things into aquatic creatures...

A makeshift
        set of stairs
             are encrusted
                 with dried
                     navgel on
                        the far side
              He swims in **graceful** around the support braces
Lojol always says   *Space makes creatures into aquatic things...*
He flips&flippers his way to the console and **intimates** *squelch!* **Janet into an existing blob of glue** finds the tenticlead and jack & Janet enjoy a mechanical kind of intercourse   The ship comes alive with her vibrancy & now she *is* the ship and Lojol prepares to ooze back into the womb!
You still got that refund code darlin'?
[Of course!]
Great, let's get outa here.

He straps the *bzz!* electrodes to his temples **the temple of his body** and immerses himself in **the slime of** the tank while she pays the docking repair fees and then arranges the exact refund in a piratical accountancy **figure diddle** fashion

She'**ll never let on that she** gets as close as she can to an ERoTiC sENSATiON whenever he immerses himself in her **because remember that she** *is* **the ship and everything in it now** and modesty stops him from making lewd comments **even though he knows what it does to her** because he wired up a feedback lead **one night when she was on power** standby *(& of course she knows! Senses!)* even still he does nothing to conceal his TREMENDOUS!   ERECTION!

ONE WONDERS if either of them

realise that even when Lojol has enough

money & finally buys Janet her body it will never be as good as this!

But that's life I suppose

Who sent you?
Who are you with?
What do you want?
I sent myself.
Why?
Where from?
What for?
What do you want?

Only one *member* does not speak

Look, who <u>are</u> you people?
We are but simple farmers.
Trying to protect our interests.
What do you want?
I don't want anything from your dumb cluck hick bio-peon farm.

I was summoned here, remember?

VartaLobelia brandishes the **dried** kelp tying her wrists **together**

And as soon as you're satisfied I'll be getting my newly liberated ass
and finding somewhere civilised, geddit?

. . .

We're not satisfied ——The one which hadn't spoken
Place her in the holding pen.

Gunter leads VartaLobelia to the **brig** holding pen
She is very beautiful and he is very **handsome** much enamoured
The only warmth emitted from Varta **however** is from the chafing of her bonds
You're purtey.   and flightsuit
Bite me, farm-boy.
—Okay...
Hey! She swings her **tied** fists in a vicious arc and Gunter **with one blow!** hits
the deck like a tonne of seaweed ——————————— She runs *feet pounding*
down the **circling** corridors blood **pounds** in her ears *Gunter roars* **behind her**
STOP! Gunter bleeding!   Ends pounding on
a bulkhead door
You shouldn'ta hurt me lady.   **locked!**
Oh! Oh, ah, did I hurt you? Oh, but I <u>*like*</u> *you.*
It's overdone **yeah** but she knows how these things work
You, ah... You do?
Of course! Would you like me to kiss you better?
Hur hur.
Oh, poor you, I can't believe I hurt you. You're so big and strong.
Well... Gunter not <u>*that*</u> *hurt.*
Of course not. Tell me, do you have any flying machines here?
She flaps her arms to describe it because he is an idiot
No. We have boats... Gunter especially hurt here.
Do you think you could get me one of those boats, Gunter?
Aaahhhhh...
VartaLobelia rides the waves **at top speed** on a single-standing jetpunt

3

1 0 1 0 1 1 0 1 0 1 1 1 0 1 1 1 0 1 0 1 1 1 0 1 0 1 0 0 1 1 1 1 0 1 0 1 0 1 0 1 0 1 0 1 0 1 0 1 0 1 1 0 1 0 0 1
0 1 1 1 0 1 0 1 0 1 0 0 0 1 0 1 0 0 1 0 1 0 1 0 1 0 1 0 0 1 0 1 0 1 1 0 1 1 0 1 0 1 1 0 0 1 0 1 0 0 1 0 1 0
1 0 1 0 1 0 1 0 1 0 1 1 0 0 0 1 0 0 1 0 1 0 1 1 0 1 /Er.../1 1 0 1 0 1 0 1 1 1 1 0 1 0 1 0 0 1 0 1 0 0 1 0 1 1
0 1 0 0 1 1 0 1 0 1 1 0 1 0 1 0 1 0 1 0 1 0 1 1 0 0 1 0 1 1 1 1 0 1 0 1 1 0 1 0 1 1 1 0 1 1 1 0 1 0 1 1 0 1 1
0 1 0 0 1 1 1 1 0 1 0 1 0 1 0 1 0 1 0 1 0 1 0 1 1 0 1 1 0 1 1 0 0 1 0 1 1 1 0 1 0 1 1 0 1 0 1 1 0 0 0 1 1 0
1 0 1 0 1 0 1 0 1 0 1 0 1 0 1 0 1 0 1 0 1 0 1 0 1 1 0 1 0 1 0 1 0 1 0 1 0 1 1 1 1 0 1 1 1 0 1 0 1 1 0 0

[Fsae§Ξφ昔兀ⴲrgfa¿#ÅζagÆÇÐđ»]

1 0 1 0 1 1 0 1 0 0 1 0 1 0 1 0 0 0 1 0 1 0 0 1 0 1 0 1 0 1 0 1 0 0 1 0 1 0 1 0 1 1 0 1 1 0 1 0 1 1 0 0 1 0 1 0 0
0 1 1 0 1 0 1 0 1 0 1 0 1 1 0 1 1 0 0 1 0 1 1 1 0 1 0 1 1 0 1 0 1 1 0 1 0 1 0 1 0 1 1 0 1 0 0 1 0 1 0 1 1 0 0
1 0 1 0 1 0 0 1 0 1 0 1 0 1 0 1 0 1 0 1 /Just what kind of show/0 0 1 0 1 0 1 0 1 0 1 0 0 0 1 0 1 0 1 0
1 1 0 0 1 0 1 1 0 0 1 0 0 1 0 1 1 0 1 /are you guys running here ?/0 1 0 1 0 1 0 1 0 1 1 0 0 0 1 0 0 1
0 1 0 1 1 0 1 1 0 1 0 1 0 1 0 1 0 1 0 1 1 0 1 0 0 1 0 1 0 1 0 1 1 0 1 0 1 0 1 1 0 1 0 1 0 1 0 1 0 1 1
1 1 0 0 1 0 1 1 0 1 0 1 0 1 0 1 1 0 1 1 1 0 1 0 1 0 1 0 1 1 0 1 1 0 1 0 1 1 1 1 0 1 0 1 0 1 0 1 0 1 0 1 0 1

[Parlez#Vous#Français#?]

1 0 1 0 1 1 0 1 0 0 0 1 0 1 0 1 0 0 0 1 0 1 0 0 1 0 1 0 1 0 1 0 1 0 0 1 0 1 0 1 0 1 1 0 1 1 0 1 0 1 1 0 0 1 0 1 0 0
1 0 1 0 1 0 1 0 1 0 1 0 1 0 1 1 0 0 0 1 0 0 1 0 1 0 1 1 0 1 1 1 0 1 0 1 0 1 1 1 1 0 1 0 1 0 0 1 0 1 0 0 1 0 1 1 0
1 1 1 0 0 1 0 1 1 0 0 1 0 1 0 0 1 1 0 1 1 0 0 1 0 /Ah.../1 0 0 1 0 1 0 1 0 1 0 1 0 0 1 0 1 0 1 0 1 1 0 1 0
0 1 0 1 0 1 0 1 0 1 1 0 0 1 1 1 0 1 1 0 0 1 1 0 /où/1 0 1 1 0 1 1 1 0 1 0 1 0 1 1 1 0 1 0 1 0 0 1 0 0 1
1 0 1 0 1 0 1 0 1 0 1 1 0 0 1 1 0 0 1 1 0 0 1 /moi/0 1 1 1 1 0 1 0 1 1 0 1 0 1 1 1 0 1 1 1 0 1 0 1 1 1 0
1 0 1 0 0 1 1 1 0 1 1 0 1 0 1 0 0 1 0 1 0 1 /s'il vous plaît/1 0 1 1 0 0 1 0 1 1 1 1 0 1 0 1 1 0 1 0 1 1 1 0
1 1 1 0 1 0 1 1 1 0 1 0 1 0 0 1 1 1 1 0 1 0 1 0 1 0 1 0 1 0 1 0 1 0 1 0 1 1 0 1 1 0 0 1 0 1 1 1 1 0 1 0 1 1
0 1 0 1 1 1 0 1 1 1 0 1 0 1 0 1 0 1 1 0 0 0 1 0 0 1 0 1 0 1 1 0 1 1 1 0 1 0 1 0 1 1 1 0 1 0 1 0 0 0 1 0 1

1010101101100101111010110101110111010111010101001111010101101101010
110101 1010110011011001011101011010101110 1110101110101010
11110101010101100101010001111101011010101111011
1010111010101011001011010110110010110101
♯01101₪100101117101010100100101e§
01100gf1011110101110Jaξφ0110110
0101¿#Åa11101Fs1ٳÇ101ra01gÆ0
010Đ0101011đ»¥§10Ç^1¼Øþā
¿¿¶0Ą±0¢~¡£¤11æØ1ĢДΩξЦЭ
ФлД0⅄юЖФλДДДДБДДЭД
ДДДД1ДДДДДДДДДД
ДДДДДДДДДДДДД
ДДДДДДДДДДДДД
ДДДДДДДДДДДДДДД

11000101011010010101010100100110101010101011000101011010010
1010110101010101010111010001011010110101011000101011 1011
100101010001101100100011 / ...okey-dokey... / 010101001011000101010110
1001010010010010101010110111001001010 0110 011000101011010
0100 0101010101100010101101001010101101011101000111010101

Janet ———————————————— the ship
hums   merrily   as   they   hurtle   away   from   SpacePlace   dockyards
from this distance
The yard resembles a gigantic sea-anemone with **hundreds of** spacecraft all
suckling one to a tentacle

[Where's the next job lover?]
She knows already **because**
she scans every interaction he has   but she asks anyway
It's po<u>lite</u>

In the Drab nebula darlin'
He visualises the region of space...
→projected on the holoscreen ***straight from his mind!***
thanks to the navgel
There's a Thoughter
only one of its kind   *that would benefit a guy I know*
[Who – Gorgon?]
Naw. Guy called Darg
They went to MultiUniversity together
[Wouldn't he have a Thoughter already?]
Yeah but not like this one
["Only one of its kind" right?]
And now Lojol suspects the ——— INTEGRITY ——— of the navgel firewall...

THE REAL DIFFERENCE ENGINE...

There is some **period of calm** interstellar travel before Janet suddenly asks:
[Will we have enough cash for my body then?]
Hopefully…   …It all depends
[On what?]
On whether or not Darg has   um…   forgotten.
Uh-oh! It seems that people constructs have some emotional residuum too!
[Forgotten WHAT Lojol?]
He tries desperately not to think of the situation but **too late!** the memory is
recalled and **thanks to the navgel** Janet sees only too well the terms
on which they parted

[Oh for Gruds sake Lolly!]

The ———— Ship ———— Shudders! ———— To ———— A ———— Halt

*[I shan't carry you any further until you can explain why there isn't
anyone else we can sell it to…]*
Aw, szép! Because I don't know anyone else who would want it.
Lojol wonders how many digital couples ever need therapy
Janet chooses to ignore that one
[Then why pinch it?]
Cos it's an easy hit→it's in&out. It's close. An' it aint gonna get us caught.
…
The Lojolian fires its engines   Lojol makes a **mental** note
to dial down **Janet's programming of** emotive response impulse
[I heard that you bastard!]

Gunter is **discovered** bound in a corner **in the dockyard**
Ragged ropes *of varying measure* tie
> his wrists
> > his ankles
> > > his elbow
> > > > *gagged*
> > to **the bulkhead** de-pressurising wheel handle

Ist Gunter!
RrrRRrrRRf!
Where is the woman!?
RRrf Frf AaaAr!
Tell Darg!

2 **Kelp farmers** are mobilized

Bare feet pounding shinytight corridors ———— 2 electronic keylocks

2 with *secret* flying machines

backpack

s with

louv

red

wi

n

g

s

Take-off!

FLAPFLAPFLAPFLAPFLAPFLAPFLAPFLAPFLAPFLAPFLAPFLAPFLAPFLAPFLAPFLAPFLAPF
LAPFLAPFLAPFLAPFLAPFLAPFLAPFLAPFLAPFLAPFLAPFLAPFLAPFLAPFLAPFLAPFLAPFL
APFLAPFLAPFLAPFLAPFLAPFLAPFLAPFLAPFLAPFLAPFLAPFLAPFLAPFLAPFLAPFLA

Two tiny **twinkling** specks appear ABOVE THE HORIZON behind VartaLobelia

She twists to see

to sea

the throttle on the stick

hard~thumps~across~ the~waves~*spray~stings~her~eyes*

She taps the fuel gauge—nearly EMPTY!

Two OrniFlyers **bigger** **than** **motes** **now** near the dying jetpunt

You have a black on your record.
Frij—the person **not the ship** *speaks* though she&she are one and her voice
comes from every corner of the cabin and her eyes peer from every nook—A
statement **really a question** disguised as a taunt—Frank says nothing *shuffles*
uncomfortable *more than usual* He's found himself rather attracted to her
She wears a **skintight** black latex bodysuit
Looks like the type that comes *as a membrane* in an application ring...
But on closer inspection he **sees** realises he can't discern the boundaries
!!

She's been to one of the Great Fashion Taxidermists
It's actually her *skin*

Re-moved
Re-**coloured**
Re-styled

N i p s n i p t u c k p l e a t s m o o t h e d

The closer he looks the less is left to his *hapless* imagination
Attr*action* turns to lust &nd his legs are no longer the only thing which
resemble Pan —— *in fact* Bacchus would be shamed & proud!
I can help you with that...   Frij suggestivelies
But Frank's *undermodified* hormones cannot tell to what she pertains
Sensors smell it **read it** taste his confused polyscentic reaction
and the ship shud~ders through space
in a little chuckle to itself

A Note On One Of The Pioneers Of The Age...

Practically every edible consumable to be found on any terran-derived space community *and quite a number of assimilated alien co-ops* uses **as its staple** a substance known as :

PICKEL was first created during **the exploration to** the concept of the Food Replicator ; that miraculous box which **recreates** any substance recorded in its database   It was created by a man named **Sydney Pickel** Sydney was the first human to digitally record the genetic structure of a vegetable ————————————————————————— the humble

c   u   c   u   m   b   e   r

So ; using   *as a base* : a slurry comprised of cotton fibres *and Vegestock*
                2 crudely modified photocopy machines
                & a computer from an old automobile engine...

His   primary   attempt   was   in   one   way   an   execrable   flop
~   h   o   w   e   v   e   r   ~
He   did   succeed   in   creating   a   wholly   new   type   of   plant   matter...

What came out of Sydney's botched experiment still resembled the cotton slurry *perhaps a little more glutinous* it had turned from a dusty grey to an iridescent green *& as he stood there watching it* mesmerised it doubled tr3bled qua4rupled over the EDGE OF THE DISH

In the ensuing *panicked* mop-up operation Sydney discovered this plant could only be eradicated through the abolition of all light...

> ...it thrived under : blowtorch
> and—amidst : acid
> with zero-g : ravity
> even just : 1 L*ED*!

Each cell a miniature **leaky** battery *a capacitor if you will* devouring light and storing a little glowing doggy-bag for later — in total darkness it survives feeding off its cache *or cannibalising its neighbour* until eventually it withers to thin grey ash
Pickel though the substance was a complete accident *thought to himself*
Well, so am I in a way...
and decided to put his name to it
Thus the P*ICKE*L **Printed Food Company LTD** was born

BL!NK   Out of ManicSpace
The weary craft sluices *sideways* re-entry systems decadent for want of an
upgrade **steering thrusters working hard towards correction** approaching
A glittering man-made jewel in the distance
Researchstation ~ Waypoint ~ Beacon ~ & ~ Interglobal ~ Delicatessen
A*n iridescent green* satellite
surrounded ***at this time*** by a hundred little satellites of its own
A warning message *bl*i*ps* in ripples issuing from the SpaceBase
[Looks like a Pickel lockdown Lojol]
| Busses | EvacPods | SpaceTents | & | Bivouax |
litter the surrounding area
I reckon it is darlin'.
An unconcealed smirk claws its crooked way across his face
[Oh dear. You planned this?]

Aside from the fights **the discrepancies** *the differences in physical existence*
Janet couldn't help but love him for his waggishness
Briefly—*for her own amusement* she devises a formula to explain the universal
allure of Cads & Bounders™ up to the fi5th iteration
$$X.Z(Z.X)^{(X.Z)^{(Z.X)^{(x2)}}}$$

A TRADESMANS RUSE...

Remember the stop on Pygmalion-6?
Lojol had heard an old acquaintance of his was squatting there **down on his luck** so he'd helped him out with : a bunch of cred$
a Pickelbomb &
a proviso for sabotage *hoho!*
She reads all this **his last thought** through the intergel before he disinsinuates himself from the NavTank —&— as he emerges the resi*Goo* leaps for dear life *like ticks from a hound* back into the vat before its limited lifespan expires
Get me the mayor on the looker could ya?
The image of a secretarial bot binarises onto the screen
WE REGRET TO INFORM THE CALLER THAT THE MAYOR OF THE HERVEY SPACEBASE IS TEMPORARILY UNAVAILABLE DUE TO PICKELEVAC
A recording!
WE APPRECIATE YOUR COMMUNICATION. IF YOU WOULD LIKE TO LEAVE YOUR—
Blah blah listen up botbrain—just tell the man that the Cleaner is here.

There is a moment of **agitated!** tics and whirrs not dissimilar to the secretaries of old before the terse reply
RIGHT AWAY... SIR.   *doot!*
Oh, thank Terra you're here!   The mayor :
A hyper-evolved human with Genetic*cosmetic* highlights
of Edwardian Wickerwork
This is the third re-cycle of the, uh, infestation.
Leave it to me, sir. Be done in a jiffy.
Lojol flashes his best tradesman smile

VartaLobelia shoved *roughly* through the door of the cell
Her two escorts bruised **scratched** bandaged & bleeding
→She's been a scrapper all her life
The hatch irises **to a mere viewing hole** barely large enough to fit her hand

STOMPSTOMPSTOMPSTOMP off trudge the heavies STOMPSTOMPSTOMPSTOMPSTOMP
Inside : the cell is a sphere
with a gridmetal floor
too small to lay straight
definitely too short to stand
through the floor she can see a **flussure**
~~~
Without any tools though *it's useless* to contemplate as means of escape
She sits **in her undergarments** imprinting the grid pattern on her posterior

taptap
at the opening
a forehead—cherry blonde wisps
delicate manicured
curl over the edge **& on tiptoes**   fingers

> a young lady's eye
> appears

Hello?
Varta has met her kind before; Kelpfarmer's daughter—never been offworld
What
whispered *I can help you escape*
So?
Don't you want to escape?
Hell yeah. But what's in it for you?
I want to come with you
She knew it **don't do it Varta** quoth her experience
What makes you think I'll take you? What makes you think I won't just use you and then dump you a mercilessly long swim from your dinky little farm, laughing as I motor away?

I'll risk it. I have to go
Ah! In trouble with a boy are we?
No!
A girl?
…
…there's a flush under the floor passes a *cacophonic* multitool **through the porthole** *Do you know what a Gammamemnon Invertebrator is?*
Sure I do a moments cognition *What the hell have you got one here for?!*
Good. Once you're there you'll know what to do. I'll meet you at the trimary exhaust.
...and gone

4

Gent**icles** usher the Voyager to a deeper hold of the ship
modifications app**end**ages extremites & **append**icular *extra*versions
Then deeper still

GRAVITY INCREASES
to the area o
f greater
habitu
ants

flick~*BLINK!*~switch
Voyager
is con*sci*ous
again

Voyager
flexes *unconscious of* its
new limbs

0 1 1 0 0 1 0 1 0 0 1 0 1 0 1 0 1

0 1 0 1 0 1 0 1 1 0 0 0 1 1 0 1 1

1 1 0 1 / Well where / 1 0 0 1

1 0 1 0 1 / the heck / 0 1 1 0 1

1 0 1 1 / am I now? / 0 1 1 1 1

1 0 1 1 0 0 1 0 1 1 1 1 0 1 1 1 1

1 0 1 0 1 1 1 0 1 1 1 0 1 0 0 1 1

a translator unit
warbles through
the screen

Ą ± 0 ¢ ~ ¡ £ ¤ 1 ζ Θ Љ ? 0

⅝ ॼ 1 ☀ Ô ħ й 1 ¥ § 1 Љ

Ç ^ 1 ¼ Ø þ ā ¿¿ ¶ ψ Ħ « 0

1 ? 1 Æ © Å æ Ø 1 Ϛ Д Ω ξ1

Џ Э ф л Д 0 χ ю Ж Ф

Shadowy forms Point & Stare
through the **crystal** barrier
of the

Zoo

An *ovi*form ——————————————————— sliced in half
PsHsHsHt! ——————————————————————— from tip to
releases it's *chalazae* grasp of the Lojolian ———————— base
————————————————————————————————— Inside : Lojol
wearing a *clear* p1ece **disposable** skin
Snap-fit from a DispensRing in the aft hold...

Snug : eyelids can't close ; *Hair*
: *matted flat* ; Testicles **&** todger
: a squashed mound at his groin ;
: Only *1*ne duct breaches
: epithelium **at his mouth**
breathing thru converter apparatus like : divers uze
but : diverse use

The shell of the egg*craft* is transparent also
and as he pilots through the **satellites of the SpaceBase** schoolboys
titter & point

Near the base *spins*–e a s e s–t h r o u g h–Pickel & adheres to the lock
Behind him the hatch dilates   Inside : remnants of Pickel *wan* **dying**
in the corners drink at the beam of his
torch If he **had** had Frank's eyes **he thinks** he wouldn't have needed it

Janet **in his earpiezo** *whispers* directions through the warren
Finally reaches the research level *remember all the power is off so* all the
SCHOOTS are dead *but because of that* the shields are *d*efunct
o
w
n too*!*

Hyperadvanced

——*THOUGHTER*——

Model:ZXX0103

Lies easy pickings for sneaky pluckers
and in its place *he leaves* a NULLIFIER
For   he   is   *an   honest*   crook
and   likes   to   do—the—job—right
no   matter   what   it   is!

Thus, with the de**vice** under his arm, Lojol
Swims back *to the Pod* and cracks the seal

. . .

...to the Lojolian waiting patiently→out of range of the nullifier *mind you*

Releases spraydroids who explode Squ*Ink*

in a cloud
glooping over everything

Janet leaves a message *with the mayor's SECRETARY* saying :
<*The job is done*> **or rather**—b1nary c0de to that effect
The SECRETARY passes it on *011verbat1m110* just before

the nullifiers
timer clicks
to zer000
00000
000
0

Every——electrical——appliance——on——every——craft——in——range——goes
1 1 0 0 0 1 0 1 0 1 0 1 0 1 0 1 0 1 0 1 0 1 0 0 1 0 0 1 1 0 1 0 0 1 1 X ~ **dead**

LIGHTS GO OUT

NeoMilk *turns* in the fridge...

...and the mayor ponders the last line of Lojol's message
which read : <*You can't make an omelet without breaking some eggs*>

VartaLobelia vermicrawls through the **makeshift** Trimary Exhaust of an Ancient ———— *not-to-mention* ———— illegal ———— & ———— jury-rigged

> Gammamemnon
> Invertebrator

...fargin' bio-hick despots...
Varta has clued onto what type of operation is being run here
...rotten shiftless autocratic nerdboyz...
she squirms and wriggles along the tightening poretube
...fry yer slave-makin' arse in amino acid...
Writhe **worm!** forces her hand through the final sphincter
& GRAB!!

Her hand is gripped *tight* and she is hauled out
Flops *exhausted* onto the floor in amniotic drainings
Hiya! I'm Zroy.
Varta wheezes **and slips**—standing beside the girl from the brig
Okay we gotta go right now.
claps a GillMask onto Varta's face
D'ya think I could get some clothes on?
muffled behind the aspirator *her knickers slid off in the tube !*
No time. Ready?
No.

Zroy hits a button on the wall and *in the moment before* the room is flushed Varta sees she is holding a MindHarness ready & The floor opens ~

Water rushes
;ushers
flushes

EYES!! Bubbles tumble around them and a huge ocean carnivore lunges to**war**ds them Zroy flicks *piscine* evasive & hammers the HarnessPoint right between its **EYES!!**

Wills the great beast snaps shut its jaws **before it can feast** & slows to a *powerful* lazy idle

Zroy spins [*it*] around—Varta grabs a dorsal hook—guides the creature down to the bottom of the *vast* cage and through a G|A|T|E She checks a meter at her wrist and steers *the giant fish* into the gloom of
O P E N W A T E R

In the greater *most important* **Grand-High** boardroom amid countless models fashioned **built** from the ancient toy blocks overlooking the VvvvvvAAAAAAASSSSSSSSTTTTTT SpaceDockYards 4our senior *elder* executives hold an emergency *woop!woop!* meeting

#1 Where did you get this information?

#2 One of my sources. Very reliable. Heard it from the horse's mouth

#3 Really? Why would the creator of such a thing not keep it as quiet as possible?

#2 He was just a dumb kid—Wanted a way to deliver pizza so it was still warm. Apparently he was drowning his sorrows. Someone stole the disk from his room.

#1 So the technology is out there somewhere.

#3 Any leads?

#4 The best we have is a transaction between a common thief and a member of the Ubor. Drone called Frank14354837X...

#1 And the thief?

#4 Hardly a no-name. Remember the incident in sector 773 with the shipment of CarbonBarrels?

#3 NO! Really?

#4 The one and only

#1 Get a trace on both him and the Ubor. We must own it exclusively...

From the Dutch   *Leg Godt*   meaning
                                                             play well

Originally made from Acrylonitrile Butadiene Styrene
(C   8   H   8   C   4   H   6   C   3   H   3   N   )   n
                                                             for short!

Advances in their *nanotech* research labs   dev i s e d | superior
                                                   dev*eloped* | *material*

Dihydrastyrilactralile-7

M a r k e t e d   a s   **Legolene**   or D$_{H(SL)}$L7   for shorter*!*

21st———t———i———m———e———l———i———n———e———*23rd*
———**t.** Started robotics early in the 20^{first} century ———————
————**i.** Entered industrial robotics sector ———————————
————————**m.** Developed **NanoGy** power system ——————
—————————**e.** MegaBlok arm devised for transport purposes ————
—————————**l.** $^{f}1^{rst}$ ©o to become *independent* nation —— **LegoCorp!** ——
————————————**i.** Megalegomania: *defection to LC* sweeps the globe ——
——————————————**n.** Created first modular spacecraft —————
————————————————**e.** Toy arm of ©orp liquidated —————

LegoCorp now control $^4/_5$ of the S$_{PACE}$T$_{RANSP}$ market

Frij542384M-07 *the ship* floats **lithe** *like the pilot* through docks to berth—swims her *thin* form from **thick** NavGel into *thin* air and feels the t h i c k n e s s of her body return such a peculiar feeling being as l a r g e   a s   a   s p a c e b o a t with no feeling of ones ***own*** corpo*reality* ———— to then become *heavier* as a person

Globules of gel ***gather &*** leap back to the security of the tank and gravity is ***shunted*** super**char**ged *smells like BBQ* to match that of the wharfzone | | | | | | | | | | || ||| |||| ||||| |||||| **¡G!**
Frij expected it *of course* and landed felid *taptap* ***padpad*** on the floor but Frank was **without warning** *whoops!* caught unawares and plumped all elbow and
fetlock in a heap

Come, Frank14354837X.

Amid the   toc   Frank—bound by mental codes of heirarchy & ***the age old***
          bzz   biological subroutines of a t t r a c t i o n can only comply
          whrr of the docking bays where 'droids
                                          'bots
                                          'noids
the daily business of   cargo &   'pods go about
                             freight   Frij strides heavy surety upon
engineered footsoles and Frank trips skittish his **preposterous** toppling bulk
          Lead us to the stationmaster.
                                          Commands Frij542384M

Stationmaster Elliyot stands proud in his OfficePod
        Over **overseeing** *overlooking* the massive expanse of spacedock
The GlasSteel bubble hangs **pendulous** from the ceiling but gasthrusters are
holding it towards an asteroid damaged Vimillion tanker for better inspection
        Shoomf ——————— comes Frij through the umbilicus
          Shümph ——— lands Frank shortly after
            Who the hell are you?   :   Elliyot demands
Frij warns   :   *We are members of the Ubor*
      You will supply us with trace data for a certain craft—
           Like hell I will!
Elliyot powers up his left arm **he used to work the demolition floor** It do2bles
tr3bles in size *titendons* *surge* **&** **flex** through his body
ForcePlate   c o a g u l a t e s   &nd   scales
A similar transformation→erupts from Frij **in electric spicate fury**
and she   L U N G E S &...   ...before Frank can flinch
½ of Elliyot's ᴀʀᴍᴏᴜʀᴇD bulk is liquified against the crystal surface

Frij holds the stationmaster's *gasping* head in one hand & **with the other**
extends finglament electrodes into the biotech enterface of his brain
100101100000Ooog—
    As motorcontrol fades the pod swings ***idly back*** to bottom *dead* centre
        Thankyou stationmaster Elliyot.
They leave him **defunct** in a pool of his viscera...   ...and Frank's vomit

A giant fish with two parasites

streaming like human remora from its sides

surges through the brine

One human *the smaller* **the younger**→Zroy ——————— seems intoxicated

reaches over & tweaks Varta's bum

The other human **not shocked but** outraged tries to retaliate with a fierce
punch to the violating arm

however hydroballistics are against her

I knew it.

she   t   h   i   n   k   s

yet still doesn't   s   u   s   p   e   c   t

or   r   e   a   l   i   s   e

nor   s   u   r   m   i   s   e

due to   **t h e   u t t e r**

l a c k   o f   **visual**   r e f . e r e . n c e
that their *ichtho***conveyance** has traced a large arc and returned to the
Kelpfarm... she lets go **releases!** **Verb:** *disempisces*
once the situation savvies but *Zroy* the fish **thanks to MindHarness**
returns threatens to devour her but instead sideswipes *& the fish* Zroy
thanks to HarnessControl grips her by the ankle and drags her the remaining
distance back to the |C|A|G|E|

Two biopeons *L a m i n a r i s t s*

await them @ the ***PuddlePort*** embrasure

5

Voyager's enclosure is   wide   **but not deep**
                         tall   **yet not high**
                   it contains   trees
                                 skyscrapers *miniturised*
                                 scaffolding *steel with bamboo lashings*
                         and   a medium sized pond

the backdrop is *an artistic melange* of every landscape on earth
desert   tundra   dunes   forest   Boston   Oxford   *the Taj Mahal!*
the seasons cycle across its quartered breadth autumnwinterspringsummer
a storm **rages**   from   ←l e f t→to←r i g h t→& back↔again
       ranges   from monsoon→electrical→hail→rain→ tornado→ blizzard

Animated lifeforms wander to&fro in *mockery of* the turmoil and
crocodiles dragonflies toads eagles chimps elephants dogs & **of course**
Man *men & women* children caucasians guatamalans andeans thai indigene
cavorting in gymnastics tumbling sprint hopping **playing in string** ^{4}/tets!
...and all in *the fashion of* the 1970's

Voyager sees *a sign* at the top of the display:

& its translation:

TERRE

0 1 0 1 0 0 1 0 1 0 1 0 0 1 0 1 1 0 0 0 1 0 0 1 0 1 0 1 1 0 1 1 1 0 1 0 1 0 1 1 1 0 1 1 0 0 1 1 1 1 0 1 0 0 1
0 1 0 0 1 0 1 0 1 1 0 1 1 1 0 1 0 1 0 1 1 1 0 1 0 1 0 0 1 0 1 0 1 1 0 1 0 1 0 1 1 0 1 0 1 1 0 1 0 1 0 1 0 1 0
1 1 0 1 1 0 0 1 0 1 1 1 0 1 0 1 0 1 0 1 0 1 0 1 0 1 0 1 0 1 0 1 0 1 1 1 0 1 0 1 0 1 1 1 0 0 1 1 0 0 1 0 1 1
0 1 0 1 0 1 0 1 0 0 1 0 0 1 0 1 0 1 0 1 0 / I'm in a damn vivarium! / 1 0 1 0 0 1 0 0 1 0 1 0 1 1 1 1 0 0 0
1 0 1 0 0 1 0 1 0 1 0 1 0 1 0 1 0 0 1 0 1 0 1 0 1 0 1 0 1 0 1 0 1 0 1 0 1 0 0 1 0 1 0 1 1 0 1 1 0 1 0 1 0 1 0 1 0
1 0 0 1 0 1 0 1 0 1 0 1 0 1 0 1 0 1 0 1 1 0 0 1 1 0 1 1 0 1 1 1 0 1 0 1 0 0 1 0 1 1 1 0 1 0 1 0 1 0 1 0 1

The space probe waves its new technopodia wildly in angry disgust
0 1 0 1 1 0 0 0 1 0 0 1 0 1 0 1 1 0 1 1 1 0 1 0 1 0 1 1 1 0 1 0 1 0 0 1 0 1 0 1 0 1 1 0 0 0 1 0 0 1 0 1 0 1 1
0 1 1 1 0 1 0 1 0 1 1 1 1 0 1 0 1 0 0 1 0 1 0 0 1 0 1 1 0 1 0 1 0 1 1 0 1 0 1 1 0 1 0 1 0 1 0 1 0 1 1 0 1 1 0 0 1
0 1 0 0 0 1 0 1 0 1 0 1 0 1 1 1 1 1 / An exhibition!   Outdated at that! / 1 0 1 0 1 0 0 1 0 1 0 1 1 1 1
0 0 0 1 0 1 0 0 1 0 1 0 1 0 1 0 1 0 1 0 0 1 0 1 0 1 0 1 0 1 0 1 0 1 0 1 0 1 0 0 1 0 1 0 1 1 0 1 1 0 1 0 1 0
1 0 1 0 1 0 0 1 0 1 0 1 0 1 0 1 0 1 0 1 0 1 0 1 1 0 1 0 1 1 0 1 1 0 1 1 1 0 1 0 1 0 0 1 0 1 1 1 0 0 1 0 1 0 1

It runs the frantic length of the enclosure *ginglymi & cubitus flailing* into the
pool   at   one   end—and   chelae   swivel   **exchange**   to   flippers
0 1 0 1 1 0 0 0 1 0 0 1 0 1 0 1 1 0 1 1 1 0 0 1 0 1 1 0 0 0 1 0 0 1 0 1 0 1 1 0 1 1 1 0 1 0 1 0 1 1 1 1 0 1 0 1
0 0 1 0 1 1 0 1 0 1 1 1 1 0 1 0 1 0 0 1 0 1 0 0 1 0 1 1 0 1 0 1 0 1 1 0 1 0 1 1 0 1 0 1 0 1 0 1 0 1 1 0 1 1 0 0 1
0 0 1 0 1 1 0 1 0 1 0 1 / Mutated! Modified! Alone in a zoo kept by aliens! / 0 0 1 0 0 1 0 1 0 1 0
1 0 1 0 0 1 0 0 1 0 1 0 1 1 1 0 0 0 1 0 1 0 0 1 0 1 0 1 0 1 0 1 0 1 0 0 1 0 1 0 1 0 1 0 1 0 1 0 1 0 1 0 1
0 0 1 0 1 0 1 1 0 1 1 0 1 0 1 0 1 0 1 0 1 0 0 1 0 1 0 1 0 1 0 1 0 1 0 1 0 1 0 1 1 0 1 0 1 1 0 0 1 0 1 1 0 0 0

But   a   strangely   familiar   movement   catches   its   receptors
—at   the   other   edge   of   the   pool   Voyager   sees   another   like   itself—
though   perceptively   **pheromones** *censers!*   definitely   more   feminine
0 1 0 1 1 0 0 0 1 0 0 1 0 1 0 1 1 0 1 1 1 0 1 0 1 0 1 1 1 0 1 0 1 0 0 1 0 1 1 0 1 1 0 0 0 1 0 0 1 0 1 0 1 1 0 1
1 1 0 1 0 1 0 1 1 1 0 1 0 1 0 0 1 0 1 0 0 1 0 1 1 0 1 0 1 0 1 1 0 1 0 1 1 0 1 0 1 0 1 0 1 0 1 1 0 1 1 0 0 1 0 1
0 1 0 1 0 0 1 0 0 1 0 1 0 1 0 1 1 0 1 0 1 0 1 0 0 1 / Oh! / 0 1 0 1 1 1 1 0 0 1 0 1 0 0 1 0 1 0 1 0 1 0 1 0 1 0
0 1 0 1 0 1 0 1 0 1 0 1 0 1 0 1 0 1 0 1 0 0 1 / Oh my! / 0 1 0 1 0 1 0 1 0 1 0 1 0 1 0 1 1 0 1 0 1 1 0
1 1 0 1 1 1 0 1 0 1 0 0 1 0 1 1 1 0 1 0 1 0 1 0 1 0 0 1 0 1 0 1 0 0 1 0 1 1 0 0 0 1 0 0 1 0 1 0 1 1 0 1 1 1 1
0 1 0 1 0 1 1 1 1 0 1 0 1 0 0 1 0 1 0 1 0 1 1 1 1 1 1 0 1 0 1 0 1 1 0 1 0 1 1 0 1 0 1 0 1 0 1 0 1 1 0 1 1 0 0
1 0 1 1 1 0 1 0 1 0 1 0 1 0 1 0 1 0 1 0 1 0 1 0 1 0 1 1 1 0 1 0 1 0 1 1 1 0 0 1 1 0 0 1 0 1 1 0 1 0 1 0 1

Were the Lojolian a dog **its belly would be sated but** its tail would be firmly tucked between its legs the part which was Lojol ——————————————— hurrying *nervously* the part which is Janet ——————————————— *vaguely* ashamed in the v a s t n e s s of space **the long periods of** travel made significantly shorter by advances in LegoTech yet still are generally associated with insurmountable ennui...... . . . .

...this journey *however* is made awkward by the silence between the two lovers **experienced previously** due to the physical and mental barriers *or rather perfect integration!* facilitated by the very nature & technology of a DigitalAnalogous relationship...

[Lojol...]

Yes my sweet?

[I don't want to do this any more]

Do what love?

[Thieving & piracy]

Again the vastness **of space** iterates the gulf of their silence

So what do you want to do?

[Buy a body—settle down somewhere]

And then what?

[I don't know...]   [Raise kids?]

Musing—the vastness of his silence mocks *the gulf of* s p a c e

Varta Meets Darg...

Vartalobelia is manhandled *roughly* to the apex of the central node **the biggest bubble** of the kelpfarm & into the obs/com room

the office of Darg

Zroy follows **meekly** — *Varta has her theories as to why*

Inside — Darg sits staring out to **unseeing** sea

She turns to Zroy   *You can get out of there now, bucko.*
The girl reels somewhat *looks around* **confused** for a moment

Darg swivels to face them *fingers steepled in trope*

Zroy my dear daughter, you had one of your turns again petal.

Varta can barely conceal her **disgusted** rage

*Ha! Nice one—Darg is it? Tell me, do you make her masturbate when
you're in her head too? Or do you rather experience pleasures of a
more testo variety?*   Jerks thumb at farmhand #1

You sick tart! It's not like that. I... ...don't have to justify myself to you.

Zroy is **and farmers are** understandably confused

What's she talking about dad?

*Ever wonder why you've never managed to get off the farm, girlie?
Never noticed you're leaving and then hey presto
it's one of your 'turns' and all of a sudden you're back?*

Quiet, wench!   Slab of kelp-grizzled hand smacks across her jaw

Dad!

It's alright honey, that was for Gunter...

Darg   orders   *g l a r e s*   his   daughters   dismissal

So what do you know, lady   *as in*   Why are you here?
I know you've got a MindMesh with daddy's little pretty out there.
I know you've got illegal mod-gens running around...
He smiles **mildly** looks at her *passively*
...so I know

you're a slave-driving paranoid whose happy little non-autonomous
farmhands have no freaking idea about the <u>actual</u> level
'of tech you've got stashed away here.
Bravo! clapclap Oh, well done—hang on a minute—
let's make this a little more private
Picks up a remote control **buttondepress** & the two bruisers go limp at her
elbows **vacant** drool she tugs herself free of their *f l a c i d* grasp
Yes yes quite correct—I'm the techdespot of this little utopia here.
Now I have an offer for you—join me as second in command.
He needs an off-worlder with **a bit of** savvy
I've some big plans for this world and I need someone of your...
... skills
Are you out of your freneza mind? Why the hell would I want to be
stuck on this mudball?
Hmm, unfortunate **reaches for remote control** perhaps I'd better beam
the Cob collective and tell them I have a rogue investment of theirs.
¡CLICK!
Bio-peons surge to attention   *Wait-whut?*   **GRAB!**
I'll let you think over my offer in the brig for a while. Boys...
& Darg shoos **them** *away*

A Contract Is Signed...

The Hunter sat in the living pod of his modular mid-millenia spacehome
safely hidden in a wilderness of asteroids   System01
His lavish surrounds thrummed with :   stellar beats
correctional thrust
Luxury
Flicks **gestures** to receive INcOMInG CaLL
Who is the prey?
/ Sending data /
flashdump   explodes   on   holographic   display
Aha.
/ Do you know him? /
Yes.   it's that slippery bounder
My usual fee with modifyers 8 and 15.   *(you know who)*
/ What? That's too steep /
Remember who you're dealing with
FTLradio SI L   E   N   C   E
Hunter Jezek summons ¡PLIP! the remote FoodPod
The pod navigates through the field of rocks on autothrusters
couples with the LivingPod ***a bakers kiss***
Jezek enters to prepare a *chonmint* tea
returns to find a message *b.l.i.n.k.i.n.g*

Jezek summons the OfficePod
it swings in from it's trojan orbit and snuggles in next to FoodPod
READY SIR declares OP

Inside Jezek settles into the recliner
adjusting   webbing
folding   displays
mood   lighting
waits for signal boosters to finish powering up
|| | | | | | | | | | | | | || ||
¡generic:chime!
because who can be bothered resetting it after
every
s1ngle
firmware
update
ugh...

and   &   then
Initiates *Protocol 2*

A collection of pods wend their way
weaving
waltzing through the asteroid field
Jezek in the $O^p/F^p/H^p$ cluster is part of this silent pachinko movement
to the edge
of the field
rasteroid **data**

Once clear of the debris they accumulate
accrete
assemble themselves into

a s e m i – m ^{o} b $_i$ l ^{e} cluster

Several of the pods had captured small asteroids on their way
which are incorporated into the design
to be used as camoflage
ballast
or even – projectiles

in the persuit *the hunt*
f o r
Lojol

...formerly *recognised as* Hervey SpaceBase
A clean up operation is in full swing **space scrubbers** hull squeegees
goopbots with those giant earlobes of mega absorbent micromesh
unit decontaminators ***& everywhere*** residents trudging about on EVA duty
Every craft

person

surface █blackened█ by the anti-PICKEL Squ*Ink*
[and inside]
footprints ***moonboots*** besmirching every airlock

What a mess.

Cruising in to the scene <u>like a shark on idle</u> comes the Ubor spacecraft of
Frij542384M-07   *&*   Frank14354837X
Floating ink is fried from existence *several thousand* picometers from the hull
it's an Ubor anti-graffito innovation
patent pending!

Coms*p!ng* to the Mayors office

...IS CURRENTLY RECEIVING A LARGE AMOUNT OF CALLS. PLEASE CALL BACK
WHEN YOUR SITUATION BECOMES CRITICAL. OUR OFFICE IS CURRENTLY...

Frij disconnects from the line **she has traced the *p!ng* to the mayors craft** &
now the ship swings with muscular grace towards it

SQU*INK*...

Squink is the *fortunate* byproduct of the C O L O S S A L space squid
Stellateuthida

Massive solitary creatures
and quite rare **there's simply not that much food out there** these beasts are
hunted for their ink whose uses range further than their spawning space
Carbon Alloys – *Fire Retardant* – *Protein Supplements* – *Stealth Tech*
EVEN ACTUAL INK!

Not to mention it's great at inhibiting P*ICKEL*

Like terran whalers **of old** the harvesting of this resource is a perilous voyage
months   of   travel   followed   by   extreme   danger
Stellateuthida are almost impossible to kill &nd only slightly easier to scare
Biologists wonder *kept awake at night* by what nightmarish behemoth might
be out there **in the intergalactic reaches** that can trigger the squid's flight reflex

Fun fiscal fact: The market fluctuation of Squ*Ink* is the
most volatile force across 4our galaxies

Rare and	↑	simultaneously	↓	Ridiculous
dangerous	↑	driving	↓	amount of
to obtain	↑	prices	↓	*surplus*

Whole economic subsectors have *literally* gone to war in the financial power
struggle which each shipment brings
~THEREFORE~
Commodity investment in raw Squ*Ink* is not advised

THE STATELY COUNCILPOD...

...of the Mayor is forcibly docked by Frij542384M-07 *the ship*
IntelliGrapples adhering to — the hull
and then invaded by Frij542384M **the Ubor**
She flashes a*N IDENTIFICATION* card which seems to allow her access to ————
————————————————————————— anywhere she wants to go

Where can I get one of those?
You earn it Frank14354837X.
You know, you can call me just Frank.
Be quiet, Justfrank.   *MUTTERGRMBLMUTTER*
Um... Welcome! Welcome to Hervey SpaceBase
Did we have an appointment?

No. Where is this person?————————————— thrusts imagram **of Lojol**
See, I'm really quite busy right now   into the mayor's *ornate* hands
He too has smudges *of black* on his glossy **woven** forearms
Frij starts ramping up but Frank *fearful of* **the carnage** *he may be about to witness* steps forward
Ah! Well, you see we may be able to help. Obtain reparations for the...
gestures around them   *...mess.*

Later... Frij542384M-07 **the ship** plows the field of ink BOUSTROPHEDONICALLY
searing it from the vacuum **assisting** with the cleanup
Frij **the person** glances across at Frank14354837X

Impressive, Frank143—   *...just Frank.*

Lojol :   *Okay darlin', you're right.*
Janet :   *[I know that. About what?]*

                Oh, you know...   She : does know but
                   that thing   's: stalling
               you were saying   making him squirm
                  [M-Hmm?]   Her eyebrow raises &
            ...about settling.   **There it is!**

First let's see how much Darg gives us for the you-know-what...
&nd there's the rub The Leopard can't *really* change its spots even if it wants to *it is its nature* **to be spotted** and what once helped *immeasurably* on the Serengeti now makes it stick out amongst the regular nine-to-fivers of the 10:30 maglev train —— no matter how nice the tailored business suit he wears over them   *What are you looking at...*   he growls to the tourists that have never seen such things **cocks his bowler hat** at an angle and goes back to the `c` r `o` s `s` w `o` r `d`

      ...but if it's not enough I've got one more job planned which will fix us up for real.

Janet knows the truth *behind it* but goes along with the facáde anyway and *F f f f f f f z z z z z z z a a a a a* **BOOM!** *a a a a a r r r r r r r k k k k k k*
s ͥ r ͤ n ˢ ————STROBES ————ᴋʟᴀХ᠐ɴs ————ᴀʜ᠐᠐ɢᴀ ————flashflash
She   feels   electrotentacles   snapping   themselves   around   the   ship

[6]

Voyager and its newfound mate: a creation
                                  an estimation
                                  a *fabric*ation circle each other cautiously
having never seen another of their kind **Voyager** in several hundred thousand
years **the other** since it's creation just *1*ne hour ago
Their instincts are clear *even though no biological process is there to drive it*
but Voyager knows the golden disk it bears is the perfect match *for the*
platinum disk of the other —— the grooves and bumps of which *showcase the*
history and dreams of their current hosts Д Ω ξ Ц Э φ
                                  The YING to its YANG *if you will*

1010100101010101011000111001010101010101010010110100100101010
1111000001010111000010101010101010101011010101011101011010
101010101011101100001010 1 /Well Then/ 0010110101010101010101010
1010011010100101010101010101010101010101001010101011011010
1000010110101001101010101100 \Yes – So\ 0001010010101010000001
01010101 01010101000110101001010101010010101010100101011101
110111010010 01 /I've, ahh.../ 00100 /...I've never done this before/ 101010101
10101010101010 0100010101010101011010100101010100010100101010 1
100010101010110110101101010 1 \Do not worry\ 10101000101011010001 01
01010001010010010101010 1 \It is new to me also\ 0101010101010101010101
01001010101010100101001110110101110011010100101010101010101100
0111001010101010101001101001001010101110000010101110010

Their mating is tentative and fumbling yet sweet and kind and gentle

The attack kernels wrap their tentacles around the Lojolian **cuddling the craft** like a wrestler *they look like ticks* **on a hound** dragging it out of low-manicspace before ——————————————————————
!!   P   U   L   S   E   !!
—————————— they nullify the *larger* ship's propulsion & *guidance* software

INSIDE: oh no!   frantic action as
    Lojol   *verdammt!*   bouncing around the cockpit
   &   Janet   [Help!]   searching through the mainframe
                            looking for a means of
                       e   s   c   a   p   e
                 [But their actions are for naught]

The kernels SPIN up their engines
and steer the captive craft
towards *the distant planet*
hanging around which
in the loosest orbit
the monolith of
The Cob

Seated   at   *around*   the   opulent   faux OAK table
All smiles and broad sweeping gestures ——————————————The Mayor
to his right & **equally as** comfortable ——————————————— Frank
diametrically opposed in *both* seating and disposition ——————————— Frij
and opposite the Mayor *equally as uncomfortable*

        perhaps due to the slowtime confines
of the android shell she wears   *or*   *maybe*   *the*   *corsetry*
that the shell wears around it
the assistant and *sometimes* concubine ——————————————The SECRETARY

The candelabra glares anachronism upon the scene as servbots bustle about
clattering corningware, glinting off the Mayor's **built-in** monocle

    ...really should think about it old chap
    find yourself a nice...   ...constituency winkwink
    and settle in to the life of politics.
He motions to the surrounds   **Frij rolls her eyes**   the SECRETARY sees **smirks**
I think Frank is rather invested with the Ubor Mr Mayor.
Pfui! Ubor! No offence, but you could
    do so much more for a community Frank
    and please — turning to Frij *— call me Cornelius.*
The SECRETARY coughs **politely** ushering a new layer of awkwardness to the
setting *to which Frank is oblivious* spooning himself **another** serve of jellied
PICKELtongue

Hidden In Orbit...

Around SpacePlace station the Hunter's craft folds into a tighter configuration *external holographic displays* power up cloaking the assortment of parts in **the dressings of** a rather drab runabout **innocuous** *unremarkable* before a p p r o a c h i n g [the Dock] Jezek *the assasin* boards the station in the guise of a semi-wealthy retiree and makes his way to [the Bar]

Step e1ne ——————— **his queries are** politely **subtle**   a nephew of his
Find the Target   the wayward prodigal
                                                      his mother my sister worried
                                                                have you seen?

Stage 2wo ——————— accesses the security cameras **sees**   [the Punch]
Confirm   [the Flight]
                                                                     [the Disk]
                                                               of [the Theft]
——————————————— Out of *professional* curiosity finds ————— [the Kid]
because it's always good to have a little insurance against one's employers and discovers what the kerfuffle is about   **[the Tech!]**

Part thr3e ——————— Finishes his investigations of Lojol   *poor* boy
Identity Cleanup   such a *sweet* lad
                                                       his mother will be *so* happy

And That's What Makes A Successful Hunter

Embarks and ships off *both* *he* *and* his craft shedding their disguises

She's back in the same jail cell *genuine legitimate concern grips her now* because she knows that this is not just any holding pen but is actually a
b *i* o – d é s a s s e m b l e u r
for the Invertebrator *good biological material ain't cheap y'know* and a real live complex nucleotide person is worth 4our tonnes of raw kelp at the inlet

She sits and she stews **the rough grating of the floor** again uncomfortable
Think Varta, think! beneath her
No princess of the tower is gonna come help you this time.
Zroy's got her *own* merde to process <u>thanks to you</u> Varta
So what have you got?
No tools.
No guards to bribe.
Thankfully they gave you some pants.
Vervloek!

. . .
Really there's nothing.
Darg is gonna melt you down to make more slaves.
Except he won't She realises
he needs you it's lonely at the top
he offered you a job and like all of us
maybe you should take it. he can't do it alone

Varta *sighing* gestures at the **mechanical** eyeball in the corner of the room

Ugh. I hate the Snatch & Detain detail.
I hear ya.
Galangal and Rebus synchronise their KERNELCRAFT autothrusters
It's all "Oh no! You got the wrong guy".
Yep. It's the worst...
Helmets on *suitcoms live* **GoopGuns loaded** they breach the hull
Who's the target? of the Lojolian
Defector. Vartalobelia – you know her?
Trudging through the dark corridors of the **derelict** craft
HelmDisplay shows her pic
Nah. She one of Dargs 'social helpers'?
I wish. Pilot. Good one apparently. Paying off a time-debt I heard.
Paying off a time-debt is a euphemism *a nice way of saying* **press-ganged**
Too bad. How'd they find her?
Facial recognition. SpaceBook profile of the boyfriend. This is his boat.
Aha! Now it becomes clear *Janet has been mistaken for Varta* **remember one**
is a copy of the other but the *software* doesn't realise that...
Ha! Profile pics.
Gets 'em every time.
POOM!POOM! Lojol *darting from one doorway to the next* is caught by the blobs
of GOOP *projected into the far wall* and is held there **stuck fast!**
It's not her.
Well keep lookin', Gee...

GOOP **Ballistic Security Glue** was developed for martial use within spacecraft

the	cold	hard	vacuum	of	space	is	unforgivingly
hungry	for	the	atmosphere	in	your		ship

& when any hole in the hull *the bubble TOIL AND TROUBLE of your existence* is a danger then standard projectile bullets are an understandable <u>no-no</u>

Various attempts at solving the problem of policing in space were attempted

'tasers   would knock out other electrics

rubber bullets   *the ricochet!*

lasers   just ended up slicing perps apart

and-oh!-the cleanup...

Eventually with the rise of SL!METECH the solution was elegantly simple

Shoot a big blob of glue at your target*!*

in low-G it would knock them over *adhering them* to the nearest bulkhead

Several ballistic glue companies sprung up but eventually GOOP became the dominant market share **not because their product was any more or less special than their competitors but** because the R&D department devoted just as much time to making the guns look good ***so awesome!*** that nobody wanted to be seen using anything else ———————————— **humans are so simple**

The compound of GOOP is one of the galaxy's closest guarded secrets *because with the glue you need the solvent right?* and every crim in the system wants those keys...

Zroy storms into the Obs/Com bubble

What was that lady talking about dad?

Which lady is that poppet?

The one you have currently locked up!

Oh, yes peers at a screen *Vartalobelia. Nasty off-worlder.*

To rhyme with: Nothing but Trouble

You don't need to worry about anything she says.

I AM worried about the things she said. I know about the shady junk you got going on here but she doesn't know the half of it! *and I've been letting it slide,* **for the good of the community**

but right now I want you to answer me this.

here it comes

Have I been... *...have you...* *...modified me?*

Which stops Darg in his tracks ════════════════
═══════════════════ because you see what he had been doing *to his daughter* wasn't technically gaslighting it was something else **call it tinkering if you will** because the reality is that Zroy is yet another Product of the Invertebrator **tweaked** *to have a regular growth rate* to learn at a standard pace *to have unfiltered emotions* to be a fully autonomous person upon which to bestow his legacy to grow and learn and run the farm into the future *But something happened along the way* children are scary in their recklessness so he installed the MindMesh and eventually *inexorably* a paternal **d e s p o t i s m** took over their relationship... And so *wracked with guilt* he tells her **the truth**

Gunter *knows* things ———————— yep
                                    not *many* things
                                he can't ——————————— *literally*
                                      not wired that way

But nature has a passion for breaking order
and in the limited **engineered** capacity of his reason
he puts 2 —— *new workers* —— and 2 —— *Ich bin arbeiter* —— 2gether
and   realises   **epiphany!**   he   is   basically   repurposed   kelp
                         Was zum Teufel!
                                He has to concentrate —— **hard**
but is able to hold the thought and *here's the bit where chaos prevails* comes
to a b1nary c0nclusion *not enough gray matter for grey areas 010~*
           I will ask Zroy. Who has Ideas.
                    . . . . slaps his thigh and heads off
                      . . . .   with purpose
                     . . . .
                   Stops
                      . . .
                       . .
                       .
           Ha! Gunter did it!   −epiphany #2!

                                      ...and triumphantly continues

That   sits   innocent   in   a   *forgotten*   corner   of   the   farm
part of the **vast** matrix of struts and spheres that make up its floating blanket
upon the ocean
It is the lowest level of a **derelict** goods storage bubble on the perimeter
filled   with   the   accumulated   *youth*enalia   of   a   child's   cubby
artworks   knick-knacks   *geegaws*   *candles*
driftwoods

Zroy lounges on a plumply busted sofa   empty bottles
idly stewing her *teenage* disillusionment   h a r p o o n s !
by designing a /F̶/A̶/R̶/A̶/D̶/A̶/Y̶/ cage for her private nook

A movement by the portal catches her eye   It's Gunter
Gunter! What are you doing here?   She thought
Is your secret place.   no
*Inst*dignance   *Apparently not.*   -one knew
You come here when upset. I know ist private.
WHO else knows?
No one. Only me. Darg send me to refurbish. I find   gestures the room
tell him is not possible fix up. It stays for you.
Oh, Gunter.   She sobs
And between the tears
tells him **every**thing she learned
from Darg's *horrible* c o n f e s s i o n

...to a bulkhead of *his own* paralysed craft ——————— Lojol struggles and tugs against the G<u>oo</u>p adhering him *by the shoulder* and hands **bound once captured** then pressed onto the same blob by his assailant *Captain gottverdammt corn!*
Recognised the Cob Collective uniform *pinned to the wall like an ungainly bug* he   s   t   r   a   i   n   s   and   sweats a vein bulges on his forehead &   *¡p*OIN*t!*   manages to get a finger free
Thank crud for that.   and scratches *his nose*
tears of relief
now to the real work —— cranes his neck —— r e a c h e s **with his chin** towards the *released* digit his jaw works fiercely the tendons in his neck stretch ***& scream*** as   he   forces   the   finger   down   his   throat

> Biological *bilelogical* fact: Human bile *and its associated salts* will break down G<u>oo</u>p ***as a legal requirement*** in the occurance of the product covering the mouth during apprehension *Subclause42*
> It   is   no   coincidence   that   G<u>oo</u>p   is   tinted   green due   to   the   *biliverdin   used   in   its*   production

Thus ————————————— Lojol —— stinking ***and stained*** *with his own vomit* staggers away from his capture right at the moment that the Lojolian is <u>DETAINED</u> ***clamped down*** in the Cob's Visitor Craft hangar   [MIND YOUR]
[STEP PLEASE!]
[*--Management.*]

An Unsubtle Click...

...is the only response to Vartalobelia's signal to Darg **behind the
security camera**
it is the sound of : the lock *holding her imprisoned* releasing
but worse than that ; it's the sound of Varta's disappointment in herself
selling out once again | always on the back foot

She forces the Sphincdør open and steps out **stretching** after the cramped
confines of the disassembler to find no-one *no peons or Darg or anything*
The door to the room she's now in also *audibly* unlatches and she realises this
is a test **for Darg has gone full despot** and it's designed to show her
HE HAS ALL THE POWER

You know what? she thinks to herself *Scheiß Drauf!*
Dammit Varta — you've escaped before
this isn't a cop-out ———— this is the next step
As she opens the next door she turns **grins** and displays the rudest hand
gesture in the galaxy to the camera then *calmly* heads for the sea door at the
underside of the pod

Waiting for her there *in the pool* **circling** with lazy menace **a pair of sharks**
somehow controlled SHE KNOWS by Darg for situations exactly like this...

Well.

Thus she makes her way
to Darg's office

...as Zroy and Gunter approach the UnterFontäne of the **chief** bubble
shoo them away
¡bop! playfully on the nose
they circle once more for scratches behind the dorsal
which the man
child
man*child* gives willingly before breaching *the surface of* the pool
UNSEEN IRONY: The door closing behind Varta!

They make their way *syruptitious* to the AIRLOADING dock

There they find a shipment ready to dispatch contained in LEGO MEGABARRELS
and inside G<u>OO</u>P cartridges; or rather GÜP c a r t r i d g e s
and also **Bodies!** Unstarted *p e o n s*
but really *Hrmm* 'social *h e l p e r s* '
which is a euphemism for **p r o s t i t u t e s**

Zroy checks the contents and they haul one of the barrels off
with an Ezy-G transporter replacing it with an **empty**

You get in this one Gunter, I'll get in the next.
Shoves an air canister in with him

Consider this

diteration : : 7274981011010

[7]

Voyager sits *haunches!* in its little world
Its offspring *the product of {his} coupling* clamber over *& around*
replications ***slightly variated*** and precisely 33⅓% smaller
The young beings transmit *unabashed* joy at existence
And Voyager & its mate   *let's call it* **Amicréé**
enjoy the *frenetic* warmth of new life

```
1 1 0 1 0 1 1 0 1 0 1 1 1 0 1 1 1 0 1 0 1 0  1 0 1 1 0 0 0 1 0 0 1 0 1 0 1 1 0 1 0 0 1 0 1 0 1 0 0 0 1 0 1 0 0 1 1
0 1 0 1 0 1 0 1 0 0 1 0 1 0 1 0 1 1 0 1 1 0 1 0 1 1 0 0 1 0 1 0 0 1 0 1 0 1 0 1 0 1 0 1 0 1 0 1 1 0 0 0 1 0 0 1 0
1 0 1 1 0 1 1 1 0 1 0 1 0 0 1 1 0 1 0 /Partnership and Parenthood/ 1 0 0 1 0 1 0 1 0 1 0 1 0 0 1 0 1 0
1 0 1 1 0 1 0 1 0 1 0 1 1 1 0 1 0 0 1 1 0 /That escalated quickly/ 1 0 1 1 0 1 1 1 0 1 0 1 0 1 1 0 0 1 1 0
1 0 1 0 1 0 1 0 1 0 1 0 1 0 1 0 1 0 1 0 1 0 1 0 1 0 1 1 0 1 0 1 0 1 1 0 1 0 1 0 1 1 0 1 0 1 0 0 1 0 0 1 1 0 1 0 1
0 1 0 1 0 1 0 1 1 0 0 1 1 0 1 1 1 1 0 0 1 0 1 1 1 1 0 1 0 1 1 0 1 1 0 1 1 1 0 1 1 1 0 1 0 1 1 1 0 1 0 1 0 0 1 1 1 0
1 1 0 1 0 0 0 1 0 1 0 1 1 0 0 0 1 0 1 \Oui mon amour, n'est-ce pas\ 1 0 1 1 0 0 1 0 1 1 1 1 0 1 0 1 1 0
1 0 1 1 1 0 1 1 1 0 1 0 1 1 0 0 1 0 1 0 0 \waarheen jy op pad was\ 1 1 1 1 1 0 1 0 1 0 1 0 1 0 1 0 1 0 1
0 1 0 1 0 1 1 0 1 1 0 0 1 0 1 1 1 0 1 0 1 1 0 1 \die ganze Zeit?\ 0 1 1 1 0 1 1 1 0 1 0 1 0  1 0 1 1 0 0 0 1
0 0 1 0 1 0 1 1 0 1 1 1 0 1 0 1 0 1 1 1 1 0 1 0 1 0 0 1 0 1 0 1 0 1 1 0 1 0 0 1 0 1 0 1 0 0 0 1 0 1 0 0 1 0 1 0 1
0 1 0 1 0 0 1 0 1 0 1 0 1 1 0 1 1 0 1 0 1 1 0 0 1 0 1 0 0 1 0 1 0 1 0 1 0 1 0 1 0 1 0 1 1 0 0 0 1 0 0 1 0 1 0 1 1
0 1 1 1 0 1 0 1 0 1 1 1 0 1 0 1 0 0 1 0 1 0 0 1 1 0 0 1 1 0 1 1 0 0 1 0 1 0 0 1 0 1 0 1 0 1 0 0 1 0 1 0 1 0
1 1 1 0 1 0 1 0 1 0 1 0 1 0 1 0 1 1 0 0 1 1 1 0 1 1 0 0 1 1 0 1 0 1 1 0 1 1 1 0 1 0 1 0 1 1 1 1 0 1 0 1 0 0 1
0 0 1 1 0 1 0 1 0 1 0 1 1 0 0 /You know, I'd never really thought about it/ 1 1 0 1 1 1 1 0 0 1 0 1 1
1 1 0 1 1 1 0 1 1 1 0 1 1 0 1 1 1 0 1 0 1 1 1 0 1 0 1 0 0 1 1 1 0 1 0 1 0 1 0 0 1 0 1 0 1 1 0 1 1 0 0 1 0 1 1 1
1 0 1 0 1 1 0 1 0 1 1 1 0 1 1 1 0 1 0 1 1 1 0 1 0 1 0 0 1 1 1 1 0 1 0 1 0 1 0 1 0 1 0 1 0 1 0 1 0 1 1 0 1 1
0 0 1 0 1 1 1 1 0 1 0 1 1 0 1 1 1 1 0 1 1 1 0 1 0 1 0 \...\ 1 0 1 1 0 0 0 1 0 0 1 0 1 0 1 1 0 1 1 1 0 1 0 1 0 1
1 1 1 0 1 0 1 0 0 1 0 1 0 1 0 1 1 0 1 0 0 1 0 0 1 0 0 /.../ 0 1 0 1 0 0 1 0 1 0 1 0 1 0 1 0 0 1 0 1 0 1 0 1 1 0
1 1 0 1 0 1 1 0 0 1 0 1 0 0 1 0 1 0 1 0 1 0 1 0 1 0 1 0 1 1 0 0 0 1 0 0 1 0 1 0 1 1 0 1 1 1 0 1 0 1 0 1 1 1 1 0 1
0 0 0 1 0 1 0 1 0 1 0 1 0 0 1 0 1 0 1 0 1 1 0 1 1 0 0 1 1 0 0 1 0 1 0 0 1 0 1 0 1 0 1 0 1 0 1 0 1 1 0 0 0 1 1
```

A Cob Collective paired *atmospheric* kernel gently lowers itself
into a vacant paddock of the KelpFarm
This paddock is kept **permanently** clear to allow for this sort of thing
Huge　　　c　　o　　u　　g　　h　　s　　　of　　steam　　linger　　as
the　　kernels　　settle　　on　　their　　*popped*　　pontoons
 # u l t r a b u o y a n c e ! #

Galangal & Rebus————————————————————dogsbodies
unfurl the gangway *ausgang* to the adjacent bubble　　　　　　buddies
as the slice of dome wall *ceiling?* retracts to receive it　　　　lackeys
They've come to collect the current order *the cargo* for **the Cob**
　　　　　...there is a standing order with Darg for GüP and 'Helpers'

Halfway through the transfer of barrels Vartalobelia shows up
She's been assigned to the business end of the conveyance and
as she steps into the dockyard several things happen simultaneously:
Galangal & Rebus see Varta　　　　**oh no!**　　　　Varta sees the Kernels
ACTION —————————— **recognition!** —————————— INACTION
They look at each other　　　　*oh no!*　　　　Her clipboard hits the floor

The two Cob workers don't question the why's and wherefore's
THEY POUNCE
...and Vartalobelia *ex-fighter 7eventeen* is loaded alongside the rest
of the
C a r g o

The Hunters **aggregate** craft rumbles in to linger at *the outer reaches of*
= H e r v e y   S p a c e B a s e =
A quick read of the council chambers log reveals the recent   PICKEL lockdown
Power nullification
Squ*Ink* cloaking
and cleanup
He analyses the *transmitter* stamps and **burn** signatures of all the craft
to have accessed the area   in the last month

ATTENTION CRYPTO-REGISTERED CRAFT——an automated greeting
WELCOME TO HERVEY SPACEBASE – POPULATION 201,743
VOTED FRIENDLIEST BASE OF THE 47TH QUADRANT!
PLEASE DISPLAY YOUR CREDENTIALS OR BE TARGETED AS HOSTILE.

Jezek scrolls through his *various* aliases and *accounting for the Mayor's
peculiar folly* flicks across one of his more royal **dynastic** documentations
TICKTICKCLICK!
GrEeTiNgS mOsT vEnErAbLe PrNzZ v ChChStR.
PlZz JoIn OuR mAyOr To DiNe At HiS rZzIdEnCe ToNiGhT

I would be delighted.
he smiles his reply
and   prepares   his   ~ most ~ regal ~   assassins   outfit   **Cape**
Plus Fours
with the **Homburg Hat**

Of the local cluster *where the stars are sparse* and you can truly look out **over the edge** at the maddening void between galaxies is the remotest settlement ever established **nomadic** *even by stellar standards in that everything is moving* due to the fact that it resides on the back of

G   E   N   E   R   O   N   K

1ne   of   tw2   known   Stellateuthida   in   the   system

The settlement exists in a niche industry **something between a prospecting town and animal husbandry** clinging precariously to the spine of the collosus as it makes it's way through *s   p   a   c   e*
The residents live *like all farmers* balancing on the tightrope between feast and famine under the constant **harrowing** fear of imminent calamity for when the Squ*Ink* reserves dwindle they must band together and provoke the beast into providing

Which means:

EVACUATION ————— as the creature threatened flees at bonecrushing velocity

DANGER ————————— like any simple uber*mega*fauna its actions care not for the cloud of gnat-like vessels hovering nearby
they lost 4 families to a flailing tentacle
during the last expulsion

HARVEST ————————— when the monumental cloud of ejecta is released
there are weeks spent in zer0-g sweeping
and collecting the black gold *and then of course*
returning it to the tanks clamped onto *Generonk's* hide

The Freight League of Ionised Pilots —— *FLIT* —— has many companies
under its aegis   the largest of which is *Rbot Lgistics*
               mainly because they have the *Generonk* Squ*Ink* contract

Factoid: Robots have dominated the space haulage market for two reasons:
                     No need for all that pesky life-support:1
             the ability to survive a ridiculous amount of drive force:2

Dennis ——————— 4/fi5ths original parts *& proud of it!* ——————— *D3N15*
& Buddy ——————— built like a Euclidian nightmare ——————— *8(_)[)[)7*
have just finished loading the last shipment onto their Millionton hauler

                That's it, bot.
           Let'sz get the honk outa here thenz
       Barrel clamp **checks** and switch *flinks* and green lights are GO!
               That was a tight turnaround
          They were preppingz to set off the nukesz
          Dang. Don't wanna stick around for that.
                 100% agreementz
       The nukes **of course** are what the settlement use to
         scare the space squid into its defensive reflex...
Dennis   and   Buddy   settle   their   STANDARDised   shoulder   hasps   onto
the   restraint   brackets   as   the   mighty   engines   cycle   up
increase   their   *titanic*   /   //   ////   ////////T   H   R   U   S   T

TRANSITIONS...

Are often the hardest *most uncomfortable* parts of any journey
Thus Frank & Frij find themselves trying to return to their former momentum
after shifting from ————————————————

hard pursuit of lost property *to* ————————————————
———————————————— *semi*-altruistic community work **to**
———————————————————— political hobnobbery

The pair now have returned to **the steady grind through** space
to find the thief *Lojol* before he can sell his stolen wares
Frank—thinking   *That mayor.*
                    Ugh. Intollerable self-serving dandy.   Frij—recalling
                    Did he seem content to you?
            He was self-centered and pontifical.   So; more conceited
                            But...   than content
        Frank. Take the measure of a man by the company he keeps.
                    The secretarybot?
                    She had quite a lot to say.
Witness the grind of Frank's   **c o g n i t i o n !**
                    But she hardly said a thing
                    Exactly.
                        . . .
                    ¡CHIME!
YoU aRe EnTeRiNg CoB cOLLeCtIvE NoMaDiC sPaCe — StAtE bUsInEsS
Skip tracers. We demand Visa under the Cosmic Concordat
                    ...and Frij542384M is back on track

There are three sizes *of bubble* making up the nodes *in the sprawling floating fields* of the Kelpfarm **&nd the village auditorium** along with several despatch docks and the silos are the largest

In **the centre** Darg stands **interrogated**
around *the Amphitheatre* THE COUNCIL *troubled*

What is this we hear?
Why new products?
Who authorised? Darg spreads his
When will we see? hands and smile
Where are the profits? wide before them

Venerated councilors, when you voted me into the position of business manager this community was struggling with deep financial burden.

Kelp **simply** isn't profitable

But now! Now we are prosperous. We have exclusive off-world contracts! You all have the latest runabouts and your children attend the finest schools. And how? By transforming our primary product into something that is actually *in demand! So—you want to go back to selling packets of seaweed to struggling nations? Fine. I've wired a severance package to all your bank accounts – go start your own farms. You're all dismissed from the board.*

nervous —— glances —— *You can't do that!* —— hubbub —— *furore!*
Oh but he can *Check my contract* displays it
the farm has been *Specifically amendment 38* **on the holoscreen**
reclassed as a nation *Now get off my lands.* and Darg strides out
The recently legalised *king of **New Zroyland***

Zroy is on a mission ——— searching the farm —— for evidence of misdeed *unbeknownst to her* === *its own island nation* === *by her father Darg* **Renamed** *in her honour!* ———————————————— **By** *King* **Darg!**

She didn't actually stow away with Gunter to escape *Poor Gunter—he will be upset when he finds out* but decided to stay and figure out just what **sort of monkeyshines** her dear papa had gotten into *like all teens she is encumbered with a disproportionate sense of undeveloped social justice* —thus—disguised in **rough** coveralls she pushes the levitated bulk of the Ezy-G barrel carrier through the corridors *pulls the brim of her cap down* passing two idle farmhands and makes her way to the INVERTEBRATOR CONTROL CHAMBER

Accessing the program log she discovers some unsavoury
that is: *not sweet*
indeed: slightly spicy
one might say: **salty** data that the number of kelp-built workers is remarkably higher than the current population of the farm *which leads her to question* **where are they all?**

Later she hacks into the *secure* mainframe *and finds that* the majority are being shipped off **trafficked** to the Cob Collective—what they do with them can only be surmised *but she has a pretty good idea...* *...Gross*

Finally she comes across the disturbing news **documentation** that their little floating utopia is —— in reality —— a *k i n g d o m...* *...Holey Shivt!*

Offloading *Megabarrels* in the cargodock

Dial d

o

w

n the interference static to *r e l e a s e*

The team *unloading the Helpers* declasp the lids to process the husks inside

Gunter blasts forth *Ach! Freiheit!* gasping

Asyl — he yells — *Zuflucht!* *stretching*

Nani kuzimu!? cry the stevedores

This one's activated

...kaj odoras!

Gunter punches their lights out for lack of translation

The same moment Galangal & Rebus lead Varta **enchained** through the dock

Space lady! Escaping again?

She rattles her shackles at him *annoyed*

Oh! I help.

And Gunter does what Gunter does best with the club at the top of his neck

Thanks, um…

Gunter.

Right. Gunter. From the farm. recognition

How'd you get here? Doesn't matter. You don't wanna be

with this lot, trust me. Let's find a ship and get outa here.

But... *Wo ist Zroy?*

Who?

SWITCHEROO...

Beyond the loading dock is the Visitors port *beyond that* **the next hangar over**
The Ubor ship   in the VIP dock
Frij542384M-07
nestles itself *politely* into the parking clamps

Frij & Frank disembark to find a waiting Cob envoy *his name is unimportant*
but his uniform is the crispest of the collective **with epaulettes!**
I believe we have someone you're looking for?
Frank trip-traps a little clovenhoof jig
...   Frij eyes him disdainfully
You're in luck — a rogue asset of ours was in his company
Where is he?
The tugs have just brought the craft in.
There'll be a slight delay   He leads them through a **fancy** portal
we also have a shipment arrived
from a local supplier — rostering issues amiright!?
They enter the VIP lounge *crystal windows* overlooking the docking bays
Cob workers bustle to & *fro*
Bartender shakes up a cocktail
*rattle*rattle

Frank's ears prick up at *the sound of* a Pavlovian Martini
Frij **gazes** *looks out* but doesn't see the **hunched** figure of Lojol
scuttling —————— *furtive* —————— towards —————— her —————— ship

Hurtling through the swirling *stellar* soup which is ManicSpace
is **a little** like getting stuck in a paisley quagmire
&nd navigating the sludge of this fractal trip-out is a thing best done with a
hot beverage `and your eyes shut` This is why most star craft equiped to enter
ManicSpace   also   have   a   built   in   autoanaesthesiologist
Unless *of course* you're an automaton of some kind————————————————
————————————————then you just switch subroutines to cope————————————
Of course, most droids will pipe music to help distract from the **roaring**
braying **lovecraftian** chaos that batters at their other s=e=n=s=o=r=s

In the vacuum which is the cockpit *of Dennis & Buddy's interfreight hauler*
there is no actual sound but they share a coms channel for the flight
Their rig is *travelling* just under the speed at which Squ*Ink* breaks down
on a molecular level which means this trip gives them a bit more time *to reflect*

How long have we been doing this Dennis?
Heck I dunno. Long asz I can recall without accessing the legacy filesz.
Do you ever process the notion of doing something else?
Not really. Whatz were you thinkingz?
I don't know. Something important. Something worthwhile.
Hmmz.
We're not getting any younger. I replaced thr3e servos last cycle.

What Buddy doesn't realise is that it's the *little* imperfections
which make Dennis love him more

Lojol taps his *or is it Janets?* handset onto the entrance plate of the Ubor craft in the hangar and Janet & the Ship start chatting **merrily** away
sort of like:

[Hi! ——wHo! ——Me ——TrUsT?——Of course darling! ——PrOvE]
01101000 01100001 01101110 01100100 01110011 01101000 01100001 01101011 01100101

The hatch *irises* open and Lojol *hurries* inside

                            frantic **comical** rushing to and fro & to the cockpit
whispering   *Where's the NavGel tank!?*
                     Feels slightly uncomfortable in such a modern flight deck
[The ship computer told me it has a spare YuEsBe-M socket I can use]
                   OK.   *still hushed*
        [Lojol. Why are we whispering?]   because
there's no-one around   *Oh.*   old habits *die hard*
Stands up straight   *Right.*
Janet fires up the system ——*[Let's go then]* ————GuEsT LoGIN *¡pding!*

Instrument panels release a **luminous** mexican wave across the room The ship *feels like it's* flexing its muscles **raring to go!** as its reactor warms up and *jetty*clamps release from landing*hooves* with jets of
                            s u p e r c o o l e d steam
Wall to wall screens display *the interior of the hangar* and as the craft lifts off Lojol sees the **dark** figure of Frij542384M *though he doesn't know her yet* banging enraged ***silently*** against the flightlounge glass

[8]

Voyager surveys its **little utopia**
uncomfortably*comfortable* —————————————————————
——————————————————— cosily*cramped* ———————————
——————————————————————— cosseted*closeted* —
————————————————————————————————— & dis**gruntled**
the shine *of animal lust* has dulled
and   the beating of
the *hum*drum is persistent
Amicréé feels *antennae sense* **aerials** *gain* the discontent keenly

```
1 0 1 0 1 0 1 0 1 1 0 1 0 0 1 0 1 0 1 0 1 0 1 0 1 0 1 0 1 0 0 1 0 1 0 1 0 0 1 0 1 0 1 0 1 0 1 0 0 1 0 1 0 1 0 1 0
1 0 0 1 0 0 1 0 1 0 1 0 1 0 1 0 1 0 1 0 1 0 1 0 1 1 0 1 0 0 0 1 0 1 1 0 1 0 1 0 1 0 1 0 1 0 1 0 1 0 1 0 1 0 1 1 0
1 1 0 0 1 0 0 0 1 0 1 0 1 0 1 1 0 1 0 1 0 1 \ Was ist die Sorge? \ 0 1 1 1 0 1 0 1 0 0 0 1 0 0 1 1 1 1 0 1 0
1 0 1 0 1 0 0 1 0 1 1 0 1 0 0 1 0 1 1 0 1 0 1 0 1 0 1 0 1 0 1 0 1 0 1 0 1 0 1 0 0 0 0 1 0 1 0 1 0 1 0 1 1 0 1 1 0
1 0 1 0 1 0 1 0 1 0 1 0 0 1 0 1 1 0 1 1 0 1 0 / I've lost my way / 1 1 0 1 0 1 1 0 1 1 0 1 0 1 1 0 1 0 1 0 0 0
1 0 1 0 1 0 0 1 1 0 1 0 1 0 1 0 1 0 1 0 1 1 0 1 0 1 0 1 0 1 0 1 0 1 0 1 1 1 0 1 0 1 0 1 0 0 0 1 0 1 1 0 1 0 1
0 1 0 1 0 1 0 1 0 0 1 0 1 0 1 0 1 1 0 0 1 1 \ What ist das way? \ 0 1 0 1 0 1 0 1 0 1 0 0 1 0 1 0 1 0 1 0 1
0 1 0 1 0 1 0 1 0 1 0 1 1 0 1 0 1 0 1 0 1 0 1 0 1 0 1 0 1 0 1 0 1 0 1 1 1 0 1 0 1 0 1 0 1 0 1 0 1 0 1 0 1 0 1 0 0
1 0 1 0 1 1 0 0 1 0 1 1 0 1 0 1 1 0 1 0 / The voyage – I'm Voyager / 1 0 1 0 1 0 1 0 1 0 1 1 0 1 0 1 0 1 0 1 0
0 1 0 1 0 1 0 1 0 1 0 1 0 0 1 0 1 / What am I if I am not voyaging? / 0 1 0 1 0 1 0 1 0 1 0 1 0 1 0 1 0
1 0 1 0 1 0 1 0 1 0 1 0 1 1 1 0 1 0 1 0 1 0 0 1 0 1 0 1 0 1 0 1 0 1 0 1 0 1 0 1 0 1 0 0 0 1 1 0 0 1 0 1 0 1 0 1 0
1 0 1 0 1 0 1 0 1 0 0 1 1 0 1 0 1 0 1 0 1 0 \ Yet you are living \ 1 0 1 0 1 0 1 0 1 0 1 0 1 0 1 0 1 1 0 1 0 1
0 1 0 0 0 1 1 1 0 1 1 0 1 \ There are deeper forms of voyage than travel \ 1 1 0 1 0 1 1 0 1 1 0 1 0
1 0 1 0 1 0 1 1 0 1 0 1 1 1 0 1 0 1 1 0 1 0 1 0 1 0 1 1 0 1 0 1 0 1 1 0 0 0 1 0 0 1 0 1 0 0 0 0 1 0 1 0 0 1 0 0 1 0 0
0 0 1 1 0 1 1 0 0   0 1 / But I was sent to discover / 0 1 0 1 1 0 0 0 / to inform / 0 1 0 1 0 1 0 1 0 1 1
0 1 0 1 0 1 0 1 0 1 0 1 1 1 1 0 1 0 1 1 1 0 1 0 1 0 1 0 1 0 1 0 1 0 1 1 0 1 0 0 1 0 1 0 1 0 1 0 1 0 1 0 1 0 1 0 0
1 0 1 0 1 0 0 1 0 1 0 1 0 1 0 1 0 0 1 0 1 0 1 1 0 1 0 1 0 0 1 0 0 1 0 1 0 1 0 1 0 1 0 1 0 1 0 1 0 1 1 0 1 0 0
```

01 1010100101010101010010101010100100101010101010101010101101
00010110101010101010101010101101100100010101011011010111010
1000100111101010101001011010010110101010101010101010101010000
1010101011011010101010101001011010101011010110110101 10101
0001010100110101010101011010101010101010101110101010100010110
1010101010100101010101010100110101010101010010101010101010101
0101101010101010101010101010111010101010101010101010010101 1100
1010101010101010101010101101010101001010101010101010101010101
010 00101010101\My dear you were but a message in a bottle\010111010101
0010001\Flung from a terrestrial shore into the vast ocean of the Cosmos\0101010
10101101\Hurled with a puny nudge in one direction with the Hope that\0101010
1010 001\Your ancient Message will bring news of Companionship to Others\010101
010101011010\But really is a cry of Loneliness from your Makers\11010101000
10101111101011010\Reading : Come, find us, we are here\110110101010101
1010111010110101011010101100010001 0000101001001001010101
00010101010100010101010110101010101010\We are here\1111010111010
101010101011010010101010101010101001010101001010101010100101010
101010010101010101010101010101101000101010\We were here\101010
1010101010110110101010110101010101010101010100101010010101
0101001010101010100100101010101010101010110100010\We hear\110
10101010101010101101100100010101011011010111101010001001
1110101010100101101001011010101010101010101010101000010101010
110110101010101010010110101010110101101101011010100010101
0011010101011011\You have done your duty by Them\01010101010101011
10101010001011010101010101001010101010100101101010101010010
10101010101010101011010101010101010101010111010101010101010
10101001010110010101010101010101010101101010101001010101010
1010101010101010101010101010101010101010111010101010010101010

Yet Voyager still feels the *integral* pull of <u>e x p e d i t i o n</u>

We are TAKING this ship!
But the prisoner is not on board any more.
It's the Lojolian, locked down in the Cob hangar
I know that, and if you glance at Frank
for male confirmation one more time so help me I'll—
Frank inches **carefully** closer to between Frij and the helpless dock lackey *wincing* and leaking bioil **and bravery** with every mmillimeter knowing that whatever *vicious* targeting system Frij has locked on to the stevedore could very easily autoselect him too ————————————

———————————— Heck, it probably already has—her upgrades are fine enough to include multibead engagement
Frij...
Frank says softly reaching *but not touching* for fear of decimation
Her head snaps **with biotech precision** to glare at him
Hey, look, fine. Whatever.
The stevedor *¡plips!* his remote and the *hoof*clasps blink from impound*purple* to *valid*green ————————— wanders off *muttering*
Garud. Shift ended ten flippin' minutes ago...
The fierce *whirring* **glittering** TECHNORANGE irises of Frij's complex attack systems dulled *and faded* back to her natural saxe blue
Frank gestures the boarding ramp with a flourishy bow, offering the craft
Commandeer...
What the jebemti did you just say?!

The connection between a pilot *and* *their* *ship* is **unique**
Borne of the many h00ndreds of hours being intertwined with each others
most **fundamental** operating systems

Thus pilots who spend a lot of time **plugged in** as a part of modern spacecraft
become attached to the e x p a n d e d **shared** mental space
in a way
that is *something* akin to —— a well practised team
or —— being lost in a book
aŭ —— the spookiness of twins
oder —— being high *without the fumbles*
BUT
complex the ships themselves gain attributes too **becoming**
f u z z y
capricious!

And in so doing **the pilot/craft relationship**
more resembles the Familiar *et la Sorcière*

&nd a stolen pet is distressing for anyone...

In the *cramped* confines of the Lojolian's flight chamber

Ugh.

Frij looks **shocked** around in utter disdain   while Frank
a puddle of navgel desperate to get back to the tank   *hooves imprinting*

I'm going to the galley.   **he sighs**
Trips down the corridor *while Frij mutters disgust* and fires up the
f   l   i   g   h   t   s   e   q   u   e   n   c   e

GRAB!

Vartalobelia [the defector] & Gunter [the farmer] seize Frank as he enters
We're commandeering this rustbucket.

Ja.

You can't   mumbles Frank *miserably*

We've already done that.

Well, we're taking it from you.

Ja!

Eyes wide ——*Oohh. I really wouldn't do that if I were you* —— **whispered**

Why not?

JA!

STOP saying that!

I'M why not

Frij **powered up** *in full battlemode* barely fitting *muscling* through the doorway
like   a   bouncer   from   a   gorilla*mod*   *flop*haus   **Frank   blanches**
shakes his head   and shuts his eyes

Scheisse————*Scheiße!*

Frank is released *and shoved aside* like a pox

Varta→   *I'm just trying to escape the cob!*   ←hands up
Gunter→   *Ich will nicht im Weltraum sterben!*   ←drops to knees

What follows is **the most** pregnant of pauses

Look, sorry. She's really quite volatile at the moment.

So he stole your ship.
And you've stolen his.
To chase him down.

. . .

In this ———————— Gestures around them

Nods at the ship ———————— *after that.*
on the monitor

Icy silence *from Frij*

Bit hopeful isn't it?

Gunter & Frank glance **anxious** at each other
in the *awkward* tension of the situation

[Kof]

I think I get whistle wet.
Reckon I might join you there, Gunter.

[¡pfsht!]

As Jezek approaches *the Cob* hazard markers **pop up** all over his screens
  We Are Experiencing High Traffic Volumes at Present — Please Hold
Slows his craft to a putter, contracting the pods into a tight cluster
                                                                                    and reflects
on his brief meeting with the Mayor of Hervey   *ominous*
                    Such a shame he wouldn't cooperate...

The Hunter sees *the bright flare of* a takeoff from the fardistant Cob
Preps for engagement expands the cloud of his pod components
arms ——— *!* ——— the ——— *!!* ——— defensive ——— *!!!* ——— measures
and lurks behind one of the larger asteroids in his collection
                    Just a ship.   sighs relief
                                                    so jumpy these days
                                    too much time amongst people
Jezek yearns to go back to his   s   e   c   l   u   s   i   o   n

Shortly — **a mean black streak of a ship** — blasts past *at full bottle*
S   L   E   W   S   *inexpertly*   to   avoid   the   outer   pods
                              But Jezek's craft *¡plips!* a notification
            its sensors picked up **sniffed!** the burn chemistry of the Ubor drive
                    Now this I've seen before.
Several times in fact ——————— and all ——————— on the trail of *Lojol*
                    There's another hunter!
            He gathers his chattels and **on a hunch** swings around in pursuit

Huh...   in the flight chamber

Varta ——————————— semi submerged   the NavGel tank

piloting

& Frij   plugged in

via **console**   *tweaking* the drive

have been hanging out

a*n uneasy* truce

C=O=N=N=E=C=T=E=D

in the *intimacy of the* ships virtual mainframe

Side-effect ——————————————— *enforced acquaintance*

What is it?
You spent some time on Carrier 9?
Don't want to talk about it.
Gutskeyt! You were <u>working</u> on it?!
I DON'T wanna talk about it.

Irises *flare*

ozone **crepitates**

Wuz just gonna say — I bet it was hot and...
She enhances one of the viewing monitors on their quarry *squints*

—Love a bit of a dance. Tell me...
...why is a medley of space junk <u>actively</u> following your ship?

Galangal idling	*Psst!*	*as he passes*
Who dat?	*Rebus?*	looks around
thru the grille	*Get in here. Quick.*	**Where?**
hiding	*In a maintenance pit?*	why the
urgent	*Shut up and get in here!*	clandesty
squeeze	*Krupps, okay. Sheesh—it's uh, intimate…*	*& sweaty*
furtive	*Listen. Y'know that rogue investment we collared?*	Phew!
nods	*Yeppo.*	good job
listening	*And with it came the other one. The pilot.*	squirms over
following	*Uh-huh.*	*fluxnipple*
oh	*Turns out he was a thief – wanted in a bunch of systems.*	ouch
yeah!	*Brilliant! Do you think we'll get a bonus?*	KA-CHING!
Whut?	*He got away. And the rogue was just a digicopy…*	*burn*
so then	*Shiiii—there goes our performance audit*	**no bonus**
what else	*…and he stole a VIP ship…*	in fact
could go	*Oh.*	realisation
wrong	*…so the VIP was actually on the trail of **this guy!***	sets in
it's not	*Okay Galangal, calm down. What are you saying here?*	and
like	*I'm SAYING – that we've got no recoup, no capt…*	damage
we're	*…and two ships undockt without proper auth.*	control
directly	*It's OK, the transfer was filed with the portmaster.*	can
implicated	*Good. When did you do that?*	only go
oop!	*ME?*	So far
Durkk it	*Durkk it!*	D u r k k I t

...of this action-packed little galaxy —––— almost directly opposite *Generonk*
a   curiously   plain   spacecraft   *shaped   like   a   saucer*
humming   **spinning**   ***cruising***
filled to the brim with Little Green Men
and women!

They go about their regular duties *all the minutiae* of a long distance commute
militarised   as   a   means   of   combating   the   b o r e d o m
of   a   g e n e r a t i o n s   long   mission

They hardly ever gaze out the portholes any more **the search has been so
fruitless** they cannot even tell if this workshift is engagement *or furlough*
Maybe it's a maintenance run.
Children glide and play along the corridors *their lithe capering games* perfectly
adapted to the only environment they have ever known...

Then   suddenly   an   announcement   tone
| *Bb* | *Rr* | *Oo* | *Ww* | *Mm* | *Nn* | *!!* |
the type of tone reserved for the most important of news *it vibrates the very
structure of the ship* alerting all as the thunderous sonic waves crash into
every corner **but instead of the usual hear-ye notice** a cute little 5-tone ditty
its importance drilled into every member of the craft from the day they are born
—————————————— *doo-dee-doo-dley-boop!* ——————————

With hushed excitement they all *simultaneously* retrieve their mobile 'phones

LITTLE GREEN MEN...

Long into the future *beyond when records lose their relevance* humankind lives almost exclusively on **fabricated** space stations When your civilisation outlasts the lifespan of stars you realise that terrestrial based existence is folly *moving from one planet to the next **ugh what a chore*** So *for aeons* our descendants made their existence in the megacities of space

The evolutionary effect of the environment on the residents were

NAMELY   PROFOUND

Low gravity encouraged   reduced bone density

not to mention a decline in back pain and chiropractic needs

Cramped confines made   smaller more desirable

turns out selective breeding actually IS a fashion choice

Climate control meant   we lost all our hair

which really didn't hurt the environmental filters either

and as for the green?

...that was actually a CR!SPY self GeneMod

There was a period when food became scarce *a slight tweak in the melanocytes* to produce chlorophyll-b meant a 30% reduction in food solids and before you could say 5IVE HOONDRED THOOOUSAND generations every single one of us was a little **G r e e n m a n**

One day a small metropolis was plucked from the future *the unfortunate side-effect of* **a botched experiment** by our friends the *Д Ω ξ Џ Э ф* *who were still space-time novices back then* & deposited in the galaxy next door

They've been searching for a way home ever since

There have been plenty of works dedicated to the complex interrelations of space and time *it seems foolish to expound upon what is already known* thus there will be **no time wasted** *no space filled* on the matter but it behooves us to point out that this concept is not im*moot*able

take for example   the Little Greenmen and   their position in space
                                                                                              their location in time

as opposed to   Dennis & Buddy and
                                                              their distance traversed through space
                                                                      their spending of that tedious time

or perhaps   Vartalobelia & Janet and
the chasm of difference between   their physical occupation of space
                                                                              their comprehension of time

&nd   Galangal & Rebus with
the immediate   their personal space when hiding in a maintenance pit
concerns of   their satisfaction with the time between pay increases

Thus at the end of the day *the activity/recharge cycle* the tumult resulting from this whole space/time conundrum is **mainly** just a matter of

P E R S P E C T I V E

Janet had found the *atmospheric landing* settings and as Frij's Ubor craft plummetted in slow motion **like a diabolical inverted candle** Lojol watches the Kelpfarm carefully in the monitors [incoming transmission]   *¡chirpchirp!*

Lojol.   Darg crystalises into view
Hey Darg! Good to
Nice ship.
Yep—puffs and struts a little—*She's a*
Where'd you steal it from?
Well. On loan would be a better way to
It's been a long time Lojol, what are you here for?
Janet mutters   *[Seems a bit aloof]*
                    [Is he holding a sceptre?!]   on the **private** channel
Ah! See I've got this thing I think you might be...
                                    trails away, waiting for the cut-off
...It's a Thoughter. Quite rare... Figured you might
I'll issue you a temporary passport. Park it over here:
                                    ¡PinPlip!
                    [Hmm...]   Janet scowls
                    [A Royal visa?]   *She dislikes him already*

Pilots the ship to the parking spot and it slides **steam cavitating** into the deep *regulating its buoyancy* until only the nosetip hatch remains above —————— the —————— *boil*calming —————— surface

As the Frij542384M-07 plummetted *sublimely* to the planet
Jezek and his collection **assortment** of shipmodules *pods* and detritus
decides to wait *as usual* at the periphery —— his ComsPod reconfiguring into a
l o n g - r a n g e observer
Literally *looks like* a massive eyeball

Don't be hasty Jez   this is how
That's some deadly tech   he's survived
you're following.   so long

Better to watch & wait   in the wild world of
Ĉio estas justa —————— in love and —————— bounty hunting

Thus he parks in **geosynchronous** orbit and follows via monitor
12^6 *dots* per μm!

and   z o o o o o o o o o o o o o o m s   in
waiting for the steam to dissipate from the ocean landing but something
clatters past   *Well I'll be dumned*   *all crustyburn and perilous*
zeros in on   *OMG. the Lojolian.*   *on the secondary monitor*

Irony: he'd been following from in front all the while

highlight   =alert=   FLASHING   [target]
back on the main screen ***tags*** his quarry emerging from the Ubor ship
What the Flump?!
Confusion   *You are one slippery fish, Lojol.*   Wonder

...to the *graceful* landing of Frij542384M-07

The Lojolian fairly *belly*flopped onto the ocean at a small distance from the farm *it was barely designed as an atmospheric craft* let alone one that could land on l i q u i d its retrofit *inflatable* **oddly bulbous** sea-landing skirt *sagged at one corner* Making the passage to the airlock unsettlingly uphill Gravity always seems to put the little flaws into stark relief

The passage is especially hard for Frank on his *ridiculous hooves* he doesn't want to touch the walls **but also**

I mean, just look at them; they're filthy!

Groans —————————————————————— Taunts

Just open the darn lock, Frank.

CLUnK —————————————————————— *swooosh*

Outside: two of Gunter's former   colleagues?
cousins?
pattern clones?
Await **armed** on a jetpunt to transport them in

Ach! Gemutlich!	Gunter is glad to return to the swell
Ugh.	Varta is back on this wet mudball
{Glare}	Frij asserts her quiet dominance
&nd *Uhm...*	Frank can't really disembark

Lojol *lounges* on the balcony of a guest suite
feet up enjoying the mammalian warmth of a sun **drowsing**
banana lounge & the gentle rock of the ocean *ice cubes clinking*

Janet *perched on the little table* interrupts **her pleasant nattering** with news of
the second party arriving ————————— the jetpunt *careens* into view
[...They should be visible over by Bubble24]
Lojol picks up the **complimentary** guesthouse trinoculars
unaware of the shocking revelations that await

Great Gmoogley! It's Frank! What's he doing here?
[Who else, honey? It'd be nice to have some company]
She's decided to treat this whole thing as a nice weekend getaway
Some fierce looking lady in black leather
a big dude, looks like he should be farming here, and...
Here it comes! *...and...* his mouth goes dry
[Who else, Lojly?]
gulps martini *...um.* gently puts the ocular down
[Well?]
Well...
water laps incessant *soothingly* at the bubble
...it's you.

lap*lap***lap**

In a voice buffetted by *a dozen conflicting* emotions: *[Show me]*

Welcome, welcome!
Darg greets the qu4rtet all broad *gestures and* smiles
...and —— in a **decidedly** flatter tone to Varta & Gunter —— *welcome back.*
he lightly touches the **killswitch** remote in his pocket
Gunter, why don't you show our ...guests
...to the second vacation lodge
Gunter **fearful with a little knowledge** complies meekly
Except I'll just borrow Frank for a moment, we'll catch you up.

Glare! —————— a glance between Frij&Frank ————— **Response!**
over his dead body ————— **communication** ——— *let me without murder*

The tension in the room *palpable* **electric** more than just a feeling
is actually a **hormonal** response of Frij's bio-enhancement **flashes of arclight**
to the nearby lamp *and Varta's hair* prickling like feline displeasure
Thanks Gunter, I'll be right along.   **Frank's magic**
power is diffusion!

So Frank, I'm gonna get right to it. You're here for Lojol, right? He came
in your ship and you followed in his. Something stinks right there. I can
give him to you, but ultimately I'm a businessman — it's gonna cost.

Frank is thrilled *this is even better than he could have hoped* Darg has no idea
the **fabulous** bounty that Lojol and Janet bear
So what do you want?
I want a contract with the Ubor; Century settlement, exclusive rights.

Of the kelpfarm enables *wealthy* landfolk to come and soak up the tranquil idyll **of the SeaGentry**
idly watching the peons *toil* the fields
ideally while *continuously* buying overpriced
*R h o d o p h y t a **g i n M a r t i n i s***

...Und das ist kleiner Getränkekühlschrank.
Gunter finishes Varta & Frij's tour of the self-contained bubble
Make drink und relax. See balcony ist here.
outside Zroy waves up to them **beaming**
ACH! I go now!
leaps over the edge & lands **like a fist** in the water
swims swiftly over and into her embrace
Looks like they've got some catching up to do. Drink?
Yes.

Z ——————— *So you'll help me?* G

Ja! Genau. ——————— U

R ——————— *It will be messy...* N

Ständig! ——————— T

O ——————*...but it's not right.* E

Nicht. ——————— R

Y ——————— *Dad's gotten into some really shady shit* !

The local star   i r r a d i a t i n g   everything in its
f   i   e   r   c   emblazoning   l   a   r   e   !
has   a   secret   far   greater   than   those   in   the   shadows
that   drift   off   *in   the   dusky   wakes*   of   it's   captive   planets
a B e a c o n
hidden close to one of the poles
shrouded   in   the   terrifying   inferno   **4ourteen   types   of**   radiation
that   would   atomise   a   regular   phare   *and   swallow   any   signal   too...*

Cloaked   in   *the   ionised   calamity   of*   all   that   noise ———— a   Signal
b   l   e   ᴇ   p   i   t   y   *b   l   e   e   p*   !
peppers   the   outer   regions   *via   channels   arcane   **unheard***   that   a   thing
a technogyre has been discovered
we all know what it is
it is the *hijacked* design
that   sits   in   the   core   of   Janet's   processing   store
and as all data in the system is **violated** *monitored* it is tested
weighed
judged
by the beacon by   the   measure   of   those   listening   *Who's   listening?*
none other than the Little Green Men *and women* who have been yearning for
all the while   their home

Is this the news for which they have been *so patiently* searching?

Not a lot can get through **the *eclectic* radio carnage of** ManicSpace but using a TransmissionScrew *inside a* BeamSheath it can be done the whole process is **messy** notably less than reliabl**e** not to mention f a b u l o u s l y expensiv**e** so it's a pretty rare occurance *saved for coms of the highest importanc**e*** thus it comes as a complete surprise to Dennis & Buddy when th**e**

*[P]*acketed   ¡PROD!
  *[R]*ecord
    *[O]*f
      *[D]*ata —— they have to **ref::manual** to figure out what the heck it even is **bludgeons** its way past their *blakeyhancock* firewall

It says to change course.
'// ']' ʃ ?!
I know, right?
What about thz cargo?
New buyer.
[W7F]²?

But there's a subtext *datablock* **3ncryp73d so hard** that their operating systems are literally forbidden to speak it aloud
|E|S|P|I|O|N|A|G|E| |A|B|D|U|C|T| |O|B|T|A|I|N|

Not sure how comfortable I am with that, Buddy...

Vartalobelia & Lojol   *stand opposite each other*   Janet
between them   inhabiting the
Well this is awkward.   mainscreen
Yes.   Glances at Lojol   *Very.*
I mean, I know that I voided all rights at the IAA...
it's a standard subclause
...but i didn't think they'd make me so...
Lojol draws breath to speak but thinks better of it   *...sanitised.*

[HEY! At least I bother to take care of my appearance!]
What? In an apron?! For him?
Hey now, hang on.
Shut up! **In unison** *[Shut up!]*
because Lojol is the
last in the room to realise that he's somewhat aroused by the whole situation
it's been a long time between drinks **if you know what I mean** and here he is
confronted by a social dilemma so rare ***I mean what are the chances given the
size of the galaxy*** that only t3ree obscure research papers have addressed it
Janet's read them of course & Lojol is displaying *distinct* signs of
the piece published by the **P**sychosexual
Societal
Disruption
Digest   [Really Nicheian Publishing Pty Ltd]

...that Lojol finds himself in is **obviously —— to an outside view** completely preposterous he feels that because he has lived with a *digitised* version of Varta that he knows her *and by extension that* she knows him

Intellectually he is aware that there is no feedback loop between the copy and the original but *their similarity of appearance* simply tricks his *evolved* simian brain into disregarding this fact

Several million years of evolutionary dice-rolls *whilst seriously inefficient* is still a solid form of programming **thus** **like any mammal in the rut** his biological imperative is to choose the most viable mate

in this case

it chooses the physical over the virtual
the real over the ideal
while his reason attempts to over*ride* the drive

autoelectrical impulses in his brain war with each other using all the mental resources *not even enough spare for cognitive dissonance* and his thoughts

D

E

R

A

I

L

The simple truth of the matter is that when Varta sold her personality construct *it was a time of hardship and **she needed quick cash*** she was much younger *faster* **more hopeful** brash *fanciful* idealistic *and therefore* a   different   version   of   who   she   is   now

Not only that but the programmers employed by the Intellectual Adoption Agency also tweaked the recording *Varta was just as headstrong back then and* the preferred flavour of digitised companions at that time was historical **that of the meek housewife** *standing on a chair in fear of a mouse!* They   renamed   that   version   Janet

The th3rd iteration is ironically Lojol's fault entirely *Janet has spent years learning what it is to live with him and* she has grown **as a digihuman to love him** she knows now what to say to avoid conflict or to lift his spirits *she understands him* and whether it's part of her original *pliant* reprogramming or her developed dependance on him she forgives his wandering eye ***but not before:***

GET GENEUKT!   Varta slaps him **hard**
and storms out of the room   **scars** *attitude* boots
and all

Janet follows suit and Lojol is left *standing dazed* next to a blank screen

9

Voyager sits in the room with an *Evaluator*
A simple title for the being whose current employment incorporates
[—— zookeeper —— creature psychologist —— holistic prototypist ——]

Ą ± 0 ¢ ~ ¡ £ ¤ 1 ζ Θ Љ ? 0 ≠ ⅝ ₪ 1 ⁂ Ô ħ й 1 ¥ § 1
Љ Æ a e 0 § ꝇ g ꝼ a ¿ # Å ζ Ç Đ đ » ξ φ Ħ
꛲ ₪ Ç ^ 1 ¼ Ø þ ā ¿ ☌ ¿ ¶ ψ Ħ « 0 F s a e § ξ φ Ħ ₪ ꝇ g

1010101010110001001010110111010101110101001010010110101
0110101101010101011O/I suppose it's because/010111101011010111011
10101110100111/I was created for one singular purpose/0101010101010101
010110110001/and now my life involves more than just that/111010110101 10
0011010010110001001010110111010101110101001010010100101101 01

ꝼ a ¿ # Å ζ a g Æ Ç Đ đ » 1 ? Æ © Å æ Ø 1 Ç Д Ω ξ ◉ 1 ⊷ 1

110101010101010101010101101100101111010110101101011000110101 0101
0101010101010101O/Of course I see myself as alive/10110101010101010111
1011101011001010101010110001001010110111010101111010100 11

Silence from the Evaluator as it adjusts an ocular lens with a manipulator
Voyager squirms a little uncomfortably on the couch **displeased** until
gas vents from the Evaluator's 2ndmost hind apperture :   :   :   :   : ::
Voyager chuckles
proving that no matter how ADVANCED the interface is some things translate
interpret   xox   convert   oxo   *poorly*

Đ 0 ψ 1 F s 1 ¶ Ç 1 ≠ 0 1 r a 0 ⊿ 1 g Æ 0 ⌗ 0 1 0 Đ 0 1 ¿ ¶ 0

1010101101100101110101101011101110101110101010011110101010
01011110101010101001010101 /Well/ 101100101111010110101100 01
1010101101010101010010 /When you put it that way/ 10101010110101010101010
1011110111010111010 /I suppose I *am* at peace/ 101010101010101011011001
0111101011010110110 /in an ever changing world/ 1010101010101010101010
01010101011101010101010101110101110101011001010101010110001 0010

Ą 0 1 £ ¤ 1 1 æ Ø 0 1 1 đ » ¥ § 1 ⚬ Ç ^ ≤ 1 ¼ Ц Э ф л ∬ Д 0
ɤ ю Ж Ф ¿ # Å a 1 Ø þ ā ¿ ± 0 ¢ ~ ¡ 1 Ç Д Ω ξ Ц Э ф л Д 0 ɤ ю

110101010101010101010110110001011110101101011001101010101
010101010101010101001011 /Be that as it may/ 01010101011110111010
110010101010010 /I think I would like to go home now/ 010101101110101011
1010101011011001011110101011010110001101010101010101010101010

Љ ? 0 ≠ ⅝ ₪ 1 ☀ Ô ħ й 1 ¥ § 1 Љ Æ a e 0 § r g f a ¿ # Д Ω ξ
Ц 1 ¶ Ç 1 ≠ 0 1 r a 0 ⊿ 1 g Æ 0 ⌗ # Å ζ a g Æ Ç Đ đ » 1 ? 1
Ç ^ 1 ¼ Ø þ ā ¿ ☌ ¿ ¶ ψ Ħ « 0 e § ☀ Ô ħ й 1 ¥ § 1 Љ Д ∇ ⊒ Д
Д Д Д Д Д Д Д Д Д Д Д Д Д

1010101101100101110101101011000110101010101010101010101010
101010110101010101011110 /Thank you/ 111010100101010101010101
01101100101110101101011000101010101010101010101010101010101

The pr1mary source of the kelpfarm's operating income _on the books_ is **obvs** seaweed: kelps   red-algaes   & fucus
From this primary product comes **also legit** a variety of kelp-related products
Mainly booze —— because there isn't a species in the galaxy that doesn't
a sporadic stream of eco-tourism   enjoy an intoxicating
and a range of items _covertly_ listed as **By-Products...**   tipple

It is this th3rd category **off the books** that brings in the bulk of the ¢₹€d̲$
which allows for _the vast network of pay-offs and bribes required in_ the
running   of   an   ⬆pwardly   mobile   small   KINGDOM

                    The by-products in question can be divided into 3 main groups:
STEALTHTECH   AUTOPROSTITUTES   & GOOP
ship claddings   male or   or rather
combat suits   female or   the knock-off
ballistic silencers   something between   product they
y'know   fabricated workers with   rebranded
War Stuff   AUGMENTED BITS   **Güp**

All these things use _as its raw material_ kelp **however** there are more efficient
sources of bio_block_matter to be found in the galaxy ———————————— yep!
proteins ————————————————————————————————————
amino acids ———————————— the _best_ source is **Squ**_ink_ ————————————
fibres ———————————— but a very close second is _unfortunately_ ————————
UMAMI! ————————————————————————————— P e o p l e

I'll be honest Lojol, I've no need for a Thoughter.
*Oh **stuff** the Thoughter...*
chucks it **in the corner of the room** as they step out to the corridor
...what am I going to do about Janet?
Who?
My girlfriend man, haven't you been listening?
Oh right, yeah, & the bird she's copied from. HA!

Darg stops and fixes a hard glare at Lojol **checks his clipboard** and continues

Listen, I got some really big deals on the line Lol, and quite frankly
don't have the time for yet another one of your personal crises.
Deals?! C'mon man.

winces as they enter the **glaring** sunlight between bubbles

Listen. We've known each other a long time, but I just can't help you right now. I got a neighbouring province trying to push me further offshore, my teenage daughter thinks I'm a despot, and I literally have someone throwing a whole shipment of cheap Squink my way & can't figure out why.

They continue *walking* along the gangway **in silence**
the gentle undulations of the ocean swell **musing onwards** beneath them
Lojol thinks to point out that Darg *actually is* a despot **but instead** *asks*

What are you gonna do with that much Squink?

They enter a warehouse filled with Güp and *a fantastic array of* guns
*a*n *acrid* perfume of machine oil
bile
and **stonefruit** hangs heavy in the air

Holey heck Darg,
his eyes adjusting to the gloom
that is a scary amount of gluerpower.
One of the bioluminescent diode strips overhead flickers with disquietude
I've been supplying the Cob their munitions.
Lojol shivers subconsciously with the memory of his recent capture
Wow! impressed *You managed to get a G*oo*p license?*
Well, no. It's our own formula: Güp.
Huh. Is it any good?
*Not quite as good as G*oo*p, chemically speaking, but they prefer it.*
You didn't undercut the regular price?
Authentic concern ———— the fierce army of G*oo*p lawyers are **notorious** for
jettisoning any price fixers into the nearest black hole
Heck, no. They genuinely favour our product.
Pretty sure it's because we made it mango flavoured.

Lojol *had* wondered if that's what he'd tasted at the time...

The MEGATANKA flips from **Mspace** *spins one8ghty* and starts its braking thrust *HARD!*

    before it punches a hole to the centre of the rapidly nearing planet
          don't laugh it's happened before

Dennis & Buddy *dial down the music and* prep their final approach vector
     I've got an idea for a business.
     But you have a jobz.
    Bzzft! Any automaton can drive a truck.
     Ok, szo what iszt?
    Well, I always wanted to open a jazz bar.

The hauler **blasting backwards** adjusts slightly to avoid a small cluster of unlogged debris orbiting the planet
      Okay.
      OK what?
All I've ever knownz isz moving sztuff from one plaze to another. But you andz me palz. I'll go wherever you go.

They arm the autodefence railguns *and grab their DESCENTBROLLIES* the hatch opens *straight onto the indifferent vacuum of space* **no airlocks in an rbot truck!** ———— out they step calf&forearm gas thrust-turn and begin the s l o w spacewalk down to the surface of the planet

Far beneath them a small floating kingdom *near the edge of an ocean* twinkles

Flipping the page of his book *of course he brought the library module with him* Jezek ponders the anachro**mecha**nism of anything spaceborne not fabricated by onboard means ———————————————— *SpaceStuff* ~ Grlgenheim *et al.*

BOOP! INFOTRACE REPORT
Display.
And on the screen is *all the data* gleaned **by his network of spybots** regarding the reasons for the current contract

Intriguing.
the data includes the **real** target of acquisition

An idea starts **to germinate** in his mind *thanks to the previous train of thought* a notion that could get him out of the skiptrace **and button man** game a plan that would allow him to return to his preferred hikikomori lifestyle
for good

An Rbot space tanker
careens past *backwards*   D   E   C   E   L   E   R   A T I NG
public manifest reading ——— Liquid Goods ————— code for Squ*ink*
origin —————————— outer reaches ————— *Generonk*
destination ——————— UPDATED ————————— **sus**pect

The Hunter turns a **second** screen on it as the *gigantic* craft finds its orbit **the exterior** suddenly bristles with defensive measures *&nd two bots* clamber out   start *a personal descent* to the surface
Definitely intriguing.

THE GAMAMEMNON INVERTEBRATOR...

...is a machine which takes the basic *constituent* parts for **complex** life and fixes them into *a shape of* your choosing

Outlawed **almost everywhere** in the galaxy {ExoTerrestrial Rights Act} for its ability to create the most unwholesome *assortment of* miserable creatures and its enduring potential for misuse **people just can't seem to help themselves** a few survive *here and there* hidden on low-tech planets *if you know who to contact* they can be hired for a variety of sordid needs

————————————————————————————The one at New Zroyland
———————————————————————— has successfully remained
———————————————————— hidden due to several factors:

It's *only* used to create Peons
Semi-intelligent Paints
and Güp a few good products marketed well mean less leaks in security

The minions are formed *strictly* to standard biological measures
no funny business means nothing stands out to be investigated
Darg actually has *a few* moral lines that he is unwilling to cross
just because it *can* make a man with 7even limbs *and a digestive tract that will crosscycle heavy metals into industrial grade unstable isotopes* doesn't mean ya should

Needless to say
the last few weeks have brought far too much attention to the one at the kelp farm and *for differing reasons* both Zroy and Darg are seriously concerned

The latest popular music **electro***dingo*beats comes howling across the calm swell of the ocean *untz untz untz bark! untz untz u-untz untz untz oontz! untz untz üntz untz untz untz untz woof! untz untz untz*

It's party time and over there *on the horizon* is a pleasurecraft **the type you hire** for a modest fee **sort of resembles** a cross between a military ground effect vehicle *and the ancient gypsy wagon* The music is amplified *through the levitation system* **because bass** beats and from a distance you can see ocean spray visualised *like an equaliser display* Dennis and Buddy in their controlled descent marvel at the whitewash concentric spirals and whorls from overhead

This is getting messy ——————— ABOVE
I'd better get it over with.   Jezek blasts off
Darg ———————————— *Oh blast,*   *in the AtmoPod*
I forgot about the tourists.
Lojol ————————————*Tourists?* ———————— BELOW

The party bus *slews and* blasts its turbulent way into the farm *hopping struts and* slashing kelp as it settles into the lodgers field *untz untz u-untz untz untz bark! untz untz oontz! untz untz untz untz WOO! untz üntz untz* Brash privileged *faun*teens with the latest *lupin*ware upgrades Lads with **hund**mods *voof!* &nd *yow!* **vixen**stylings for the gals spray out *like they were shaken* from the effervescent can of youth because this high-octane party started t w o d a y s a g o !

Varta and Frij stagger *drunkenly* out to the balcony *drawn to the ruckus* Frij sobers up immediately **NanoBloodBots clean up the booze** but of course *NOW the hangover!* Varta doesn't sober **so much as** just forces herself to mental sharpness with a well honed survival reflex   <u>*her*</u> *hangover later*

Jezek —————'s AtmoPod punches into the calming surface *of the water* with **the grace of** an angry punk spit

watching from the gaping **mouths agape** ————————— Lojol and Darg hangar door of a warehouse bubble

Dennis & Buddy ———————— float gently down *like magical English nannies* to stand **on the deck** beside them

The flying saucer *of the little green men* glides in swiftly *all strobing lights and weird sounds* until it hovers above the party bus

Stoned wolfbois *and foxchicas* ———— stare in amazement **spill their drinks**

Observing it all *via the farm's* **complimentary Whiffy network** —————Janet

Zroy *und* Gunter ————————— finish **making love** in the hidden cubby &

stepping out *from the farm library* blinking in the sunlight ————— *Frank:*

What'd I miss?

Jezek bursts forth *from the pod* suspended **awkwardly** between his articulated levitator backpack and the ***seriously oversized*** rifle

he knows that he should have adjusted *calibrated the flight settings* to the local gravity but with so many elements at play **didn't want to miss his opportunity**

every time he lifts the gun it forces the pack ***struggling*** to counter the load shift ***and the assasin*** now *resembling Foucoult's pendulum* can't get a straight bead on his quarry

PkOW! PkOW!

The microplasma slugs singe **and sizzle** the deck between Lojol and Buddy *diving off in opposite directions* deeper into the warehouse while the recoil sends Jezek ***manically*** in ragdoll pirouettes

then shots **from behind** *from above* he skews and dodges **spins** *counters returns fire* in a reckless spray at the YouFoe *more shots from a balcony* and a stray slug melts through the partybus sound system

Hot! Too hot!

Flees in a butterfly jerky panic to the far side of the warehouse

PᴋOW! PᴋOW!

`Dennis` collides into *shoves protectively* Buddy
and then behind a group of barrels
flips out his KwikkieFix™ plasma welder
as an emergency for close contact armament
with a cute little FʟᴏᴏF!
waits for the assailant to enter the warehouse *but nothing happens*

Hey! You Darg?
from behind a loader ——————*Yep*———— on the opposite side
We're the cargo haulers.

▌▌▌█ █ █ ▬ ▬ █ ▬ █ ▌▌▌ the wall *s h a k e s*

Whatz the bzzrk! going on outz there? tools r a t t l e
Fluxed if I know. dust *s e t t l e s*
Other guy; You Lojolz?
Who wants to know? **Lojol don't know y̲o̲u̲ pal**
Where girlzfriend?
Hey! Go tighten your bolts, buddy!

outside something goes **BzZooP!** and the smell of ozone
Frank bolts in through the door *looks frantically around* tries to
fit behind the loader **but gets shoved out again** ends up crouching
comically behind a too-small kelp press *panting* as **tippytappy** in come
a pair of Little Green Men *retro-styled ray guns in hand*

The Saucer *slides over to the warehouse bubble and* drops a trio of the little
before catching a stray slug from   Greenmen on top
Jezek's wayward escape and   specially chosen for planetary exercises
delicately tilting off to end   **gravity trained** *weapons savvy*
floating beside the bus   *they land on their comically oversized*
                                        GECKOFOOT StickyBoots with

military ease *split up* and started making their way down the sides
of the dome   each one   to a th3rd

Frank comes trotting around the industrial mezzanine face to face
                        with one of the *petite* soldiers   **face   to navel**
                        who raises its cute *but devastating* little ray gun

There is a moment *of pause* when Frank realises he's really not cut out for this
kind of mission when  *the saucerman*
                                                          s p l a t t e r e d
Glances across the water to see Frij   all over the side
            semi-transformed in battlemode   of the dome
            a son!c pulse rifle
                    where the lower half of her arm should be
off-gassing with coolant **Varta beside her** vigorously shooing him towards the
                                                        warehouse door
a raygun shot ——————————— *BzZooP!*
                    smashes the balcony railing one side of Frij

   Everyone bolts inside and the 2emaining Greenmen *regroup and* follow Frank

Varta & Frij

Hey, Isn't that your colleague?
Frank14354837X!

powers up a partial *armament* and

Holey Shivt, Frij!
Just a bit stunned by the instant danger boiling beneath the
beautiful skin of this amazing lady
She gently rests her hand *upon the whirring ticking limbweapon* and goes to—
BzZooP!
The balustrade edge splatters molten stonework in the return fire and the pair
duck back inside for cover

Everything quietens down   *outside*   they hear *a Faunteen*
What kinda freaky eco-lodge is this?

Frij and Varta look at each other *one of those silent looks between* two people
of Decisiveness & Action **they nod in agreement** Frij's sonic weapon still
pulses awfully below her elbow — Varta grabs the only weapon to hand
a luxurious kelpfibre towel! and creep to the dripping c r u m b l i n g balcony
when: =*BbptBbptBbpt!*=   *Splat Splot*
Güpped!   right onto the wall   *their faces a mere centim apart*
Varta struggles and rages **fights and growls** hyperventilates while Frij *trained
to conserve energy* calms her down by the only means at her disposal
Snaps her out of it with a   *HEY!*
and a   [kiss]

Having spent the remainder of their shift *cowering* in a maintenance pit **Galangal and Rebus** came to the decision *one of those dimwitted escalations of cause and effect* to attempt a recovery of the lost captives which *We'll be heroes!*

Performance bonus! whilst not their first mistake *certainly isn't an action within their skillset*

Their second mistake ——————— the unsanctioned use of a landing kernel and the final error? plunging headlong into the **multi-faction** battle at the kelpfarm

::The monitors aboard their stolen craft display:: the Saucer dropping the Little Greenmen with their little powerful guns *Hey look it's Vartalobelia!* *Yeah, but she's right next to...* the *fiercely tricked out* battlemod Ubor drone then there's ——————— the partybus with its **serious slappin'** beats the assassin with the *flying rig and the* crazybig blaster and running a pair of kelpfarm workers *to the scene* carrying *the bestest* Güpguns of the catalogue

Think it might be time to cut our losses on this one.

So the kernel s l o w s **reaches equilibrium** and blasts right back out again

Zroy & Gunter had heard the commotion at the centre of the kingdom from
the distant derelict pod *they saw the conflagration* **und sprang zum handeln**
Using ***unterwasserschleppgerät*** stopping via one of the warehouse bubbles
they were able to sneak into the tumultuous area and *surprise!*
l i t e r a l l y   everyone   the muted rattle of *Güpinator 507's*
BbptBbpt!   *BbptBbptBbpt!*   *BbptBbptBbptBbpt!*   yodelled
as they took charge of the situation ***adhering and immobilising*** without mercy
glued to the gantry   Jezek
to the balcony   Varta & Frij   : **outside** Zroy
to the bus   wolfbois & foxchicas

&nd Gunter **inside:**   Lojol & Darg   to the loader
Greenmen   propelled right over to the far wall
the Rbots   stuck to workbenches
and Frank   hands raised in surrender
glued at the hip to an Ezy-G loader
awkwardly   hopping   *on   the   one   hoof   only*   just   touching   the   ground

Zroy stands amid the captives   feet planted firm
hair *majestically* tousling — in the rising breeze
Güpinator *hissing as it* regenerates pressure & autocues GENERIC warning
statements on its little holoscreen **raises her voice and commands**

Ich bin die Königin von New Zroyland...
...and I'm calling time-out.

Janet *just chillin' in the mainframe* has had s o o o o o o o o o o much time
it's   a   matter   of   **cognitive**   s   p   e   e   d   you   see
She idly dredged the archives
laid open the vaults
intercepted communiqués

[Oh despot! Thy name is Darg]

She spied the action ———————————— poked & peered about in
unfolding *in bullet time* ——— MULTITASKING! ——— the kelpfarm datastores
from a hundred different ———————————— *surveillance cameras*

She saw the pair of lovers **politely averted her gaze but** researched the girl
the   heir   apparent   *the   princess*   of   New   Zroyland
[This one I can help...]

When they armed themselves Janet accessed the Güpinator screens
introduced herself
They were wary **at first** but Janet was kind *and honest*   *[Hiya!]*
managed to convince them **and to be fair**
their *post-coital neurochemistry* made it easy

from   there   it   was   a   simple   matter   *using   Janet's   omniscient   view*
and   the   latest   TackTechs   to   pacify   the   e   n   t   i   r   e   situation

Zroy **in full monarch mode** strode about the warehouse
those outside have been escorted in　　　　　　　Güpped to the spot
　　　　　　　　　　　　　　　　　　　　　a captive audience
　　　　　Zroy baby, unstick me and I'll sort all this out.
　　I don't think so, dad. You want to show them what you found, Janet?
upon all the screens **around the dome** displayed the document hiding
ownership of New Zroyland inside a матрёшка doll of shell principalities
　　　　　　　　　　　　　　　　　　　　　a nation inside a
　　　　　　　　　　　　　　　　　　　　　district inside
　　　　　　　　　　　　　　　　　　　　a territory in
　　　　　　　　　　　　　　　　　　　side a state
　　　　　　　　　　　　　　　　inside a kingdom
　　　　　　　　　　　　and at the heart of it all
　　　　　　　　Zroy von Daliance el Guardo di Boba

Awkward glances around the room　　　　*Seriously Darg?*　whispers　*It was a tax dodge...*

　　So, I think I'll be taking an active part in the running of things now.
Darg flexes *a switchmuscle in* his jaw and `gasps` in shock
Janet pops up　　　　　　　　*¡plip!*　　　　　　　　onscreen
*[If you're wondering why you've lost your vision Darg, it's because I
rerouted your MindMesh activation. Zroy is no longer yours to control]*
　　　　　　　　　　Darg switches his own sight back on
　　　　Darling, let's talk about this. In private.
　　　　　　　Didn't you want to travel abroad? See the stars?
　You know, dad, I rather think I'll stay. Start running my farm.

Right. Now that's settled - Why are all you jokers here?
she casts a regally appointed finger across the captives
Him!   most chorus — indicating Lojol
Her.   say the little Greenmen astutely
Dude, it's summer break.   laments a Wulfie

Sie wollen ich **pounds a fist into his meaty hand** *ihn zerbrechen?*

[I think...] Janet interjects *[...they all want this]*
Zroy holds up her hand *stops Gunter stalking towards Lojol*

Plans **schematics** replace Janet on the screens *data flickers* complex non-space projections ***the stolen tech!*** the thing to be coveted *owned exclusively* capitalised **suppressed** the wholly grail of RECIEVER————————and *literally* nothing in between—————————TRANSMITTER
i n s t a n t   m a t t e r   t r a n s f e r

In that case. You know what you have to do.
commands Zroy
[It is already done, your majesty!]
and wave upon wave *the new wave* **the opensource** broadcast from the *unusually techriddled* kelpfarm radiating out from a wet planet in humanity's cradle **delivering** *informing* ***enlightening*** anyone who would receive it

the solution to the v a s t n e s s of space & the burden of time

Above the kelpfarm *all its sprawling WetNet fields* the clear blue skies made pleasant the relentless beating **buffeting** waves of the local star The domes of shiny nacre sucked at the energy *because in these halcyon days* there wasn't much swell on the water and the StrutKnuckles driving the fluid turbines creak with only the f a i n t e s t m o t i o n
The turmoil ***at the heart of the kingdom*** was mostly abated laser*shot* and plasma***scorch*** have ceased their smoulder and are now just warm patches here and there
The downed flying saucer of the Greenmen floated gently *on a field of amplified surface tension* bumping occasionally against the partybus
There is a sound like a pop—*not like a pop*—**more like**
the sudden inrushing of the ENERGY *spent by the sound itself*

What was once empty skies is now the galacticraft of the Д Ω ξ Ц Э φ

conical ———— its   base the size of a city *well past the fringes of the farm*
         ——— it's   pointed upwards *deflecting low orbit satellites*
         — it is   using **gentle** manipulations of gravity

While **inside** the captives are being freed from their *gellid* shackles
          the [interior of the] warehouse is instantly shrou**ded in darkness**
Autolights ***biomimic luminescent fronds*** struggle and heave —— *weep* at the sudden change around them
                    everyone flocks outside into the *suddenly* ***twilight gloom***

The party gawped up at the cRENULATED
tesse*la*ted
corru**gated** ceiling
looming about a kLick above
someone started vomiting vertiginously *no-one knows who* they were all transfixed skyward ((A circle)) incongruous to the greebled kinks & ruffles split from the main *spilling light from its edges* The disk descending slowly towards the surface of the field ***before them until*** it stops just before crushing the craft beneath ————————
A ramp extended **lowered** until it was precisely ***one Emo*** from the edge of the bubble gantry **that's 1/1000th duodecimal**

Two of the ***дΩξцэф*** lumbered *lithe* towards them *one was the Evaluator itself!*

¿ # Å ζ Ç Đ đ » φ Ħ ᒣ ₪ Ç Ø þ ā ¿ ≎ ¿ ¶ ψ Ħ « 0 F
§ ξ φ Ħ ≎ ¿ # Å ***[WE BELIEVE...]*** ζ Æ Ç Đ đ »
1 ? 1 Æ © Å æ Ø Д Ω ξ ◎ 1 ⊶ 1 ∄ ᒣ Ç ≉ 0 Ħ ₪ ᒣ

Everyone doubles over **in pain** ***clamping their ears***

Embarassed twiddling of knobs on the translator box slung around its neck
Ą ± 0 ¢ ~ ¡ £ ¤ 1 ζ Θ Љ ? 0 ≇ ⅝ ₪ 1 ⁂ Ồ ђ й 1 ¥ § 1 Љ Æ a e § r g f a ¿ # Å ζ Ç Đ đ » ξ φ Ħ ᒣ ₪ Ç ^ 1 ¼ Ø þ ā ¿ ≎ ¿ ***[Apology]*** ψ Ħ « 0 F s a e § ξ φ Ħ ₪ r g f a ¿ # Å ζ a g Æ Ç Đ đ » 1 ? Æ © Å ***[Volumetric error]*** æ Ø 1 Ģ Д Ω ξ ◎ 1 ⊶ 1 ∄ 0 ψ 1 F s 1 ᒣ Ç 1 ≉ 0 1 r a 0 ∡ 1 g Æ 0 ⊅ 0 1 0 Đ 0 1 ¿ ¶ 0 Ą 0 1 £ ¤ 1 1 æ Ø 0 1 1 đ » ¥
The Evaluator glares *flutters obloquy* disapproval at the assistant

---

ζ Θ Љ ? ≠ ⅝ ₪ ✳ Ô ħ й ¥ § Љ Æ §¿ # Å ζ Ç Ð đ » ξ φ Ħ ¶
₪ Ç ξ ◎ ⊷ þ Ħ 0 ψ Ç F ^ 1 ¶ Å Ø þ ā ¿ ± 0 ¢ Ç ≠ Ω 1 Ƴ ξ g
Æ 0 Ƥ 0 æ Ø 1 đ » **[We believe that]** ¥ § Д ⥲ 0 Ç ^ ≼ ♻ ¼
⊷ Ħ § φ Ħ ₪ г ¿ # Å ζ Æ Ç Ð đ » ? Æ Ð ¶ Ø Ą ¤ æ đ » ¥ Љ
≠ Ц Э ф л ₷ **[You misplaced this item]** Д ¼ ⅄ ξ ю Ж Ф
¿ # Å a 1 Ø þ ā ¿ ± 0 ¢ ~ ¡ ā Ç Д Ω ξ Ц Э ф л Д 0 ⅄ ю Ж Ф λ
Д Љ ? 0 ≠ ⅝ ₪ ✳ ⊷ 1 Ħ 0 ψ 1 ζ Θ Д Љ ? 0 ≠ ⅝ ₪ ¿ ✳ Ô ħ

They part to reveal Voyager walking *shyly* down the ramp behind them

10

01110100/01101000/01100101/00100000/01100001/01110101/0111
0100/01101000/01101111/01110010/00100000/01101000/01101111
/01110000/01100101/01110011/00100000/01111001/01101111/011
10101/00100000/01101000/01100001/01110110/01100101/0010000
0/01100101/01101110/01101010/01101111/01111001/01100101/01
100100/00100000/01110100/01101000/01101001/01110011/001000
00/01101100/01101001/01110100/01110100/01101100/01100101/0
0100000/01110100/01100001/01101100/01100101

Voyager and its family toil the fields of the kelpfarm
in the times *between* *the* *worktime* they enjoy their own pursuits
the voyage is now an →**inward**← one

Voyager *p h i l o s o p h i s e s* *writing a book!*
betimes gets invited *guest speaker at this university* **or that startup SpaceCo**
Amicréé has become an artist *m o d e r a t e l y successful*
a couple offworld galleries *the latest* **weaving 6ix-dimensional tapestries**
but still finds time to produce kelp baskets for the local indigenous markets
The offspring do what all youth find
to occupy their *abundance of* energy ——————————— *e x p l o r i n g the deeps*
advancing material science
terrorising the fauna

01110100/01101000/01100001/01101110/01101011/00
100000/01111001/01101111/0111010100100000/0110
0011/01101111/01101101/01100101/00100000/011000
01/01100111/01100001/01101001/01101110/00100001

Jezek **back home** sits in his authentic EamesLounge *picked it up while he was on Térre* at g a l a c t o n o m i c a l expense but the bounty he received for delivering Lojol to the shadowy LegoCorp board of directors was more than enough to cover the extravagance
We have no need of the man now that the tech is out.
Check the contract— slurping a Kelptini
I think you'll find my fee still holds...
Today he sits *and*   Begrudged **fulfillment** of accounts
listens to jazz **lounges**   in his chair
in his pod
in his asteroid field *which he purchased outright*
made it into a stellar reserve   ::[No Mining!]::
undisturbed but for the *¡PING!* of notifications coming from his new business pursuit ——————— he's finally done with the skiptrace game
running hither & yon *like a chump*
/ANOTHER/TRECEIVER/DELIVERED/BOSS/
Good. The next customer is a jump to Hervey then head out.
/OUTZ?/
To Generonk.
/WE/GOT/THE/SQUINK/ACCOUNT?!/
Nope, but it won't be long before they realise
they can just distribute direct by the barrel.
/HECK/MR/J,/FLIT/BE/GUNNINZ/FOR/YOU/NOW./
I've handled worse.

Dennis & Buddy are *still* trucking
the difference is they are doing it for themselves
and their s i l e n t partner

Installing TREceivers **the nodes** *the tech* between which the Instant Matter
Transfer occurs ——————————— *Someone's got to do the hard yards first*
and it's worth it for the small percentage of IMT fees on every
slip ————————————— *b e t w e e n* ————————————— **units**

A node on the big squid huh?
Goldz mine for usz.
You bet, buddy.
We'll be able to run the bar off this one alone.
Jazz bar.
ɟɑᴢᴢ βɘя!

7433 842!

Frank wanders *amongst the crowd*   shaking hands
moving through the main public space   *salutations*
the town square *if you will*   smile & nod
Be seen —————————— that was the advice given him —————————— wave

Trips past the boutique shops *and galleries* sees a pair of Rbot contractors installing a sign on a new business and smiles inwardly It's *that* enterprise which **in part** landed him the job here
Reads the sign: *[7433 842]*
      Funny name for a cantina...   he remarks
     ...oh well, what do I know about these things.   to himself

Back in his private chambers—hangs up his ceremonial robes **from the signing-in punctilioes** he drapes *straightens* the ornamental links upon the overwrought tritanium necklace bust with *i m m e n s e* pride
Behind him —————————— the SECRETARY —————————— stands at the iris
      MR MAYOR...
      GAH!   Frank spins in fright
      aPoLoGiEs SiR.   *pseudokarate pose*
      tHeRe ArE a NuMbEr Of
      DoCuMeNtS tO bE sIgNeD, tHeN—
      Frank *the new mayor* holds up his hand *to interrupt*
      What IS your name?
      I AM 'THE SECRETARY', SIR.
      Well. That simply Will Not Do.

Stuck to the outside of the Cob ——————————//—————————— GOOPBOOTS
In the bright yellow **chunky** uniform of Cob Collective   deepspace suits
the   type   that   are   basically   a   *glorified*   life   raft

Two **lone** workers
swabbing adjacent kernels
SonicMops nudging at the accumulated gunge *of the vacuum of space*
it's not really as e m p t y as everyone thinks

::*Hey,*::   ::*Galangal*::

::*Shut*::   ::*Up*::

Rebus *leaning on his mop* looks out over the hilly expanse *of kernel surfaces*
the   ***length***   ***of***   the   Cob   disappears   into   the   distance
and   seems   as   far   away   as   his   performance   bonus

—————————— He sighs **heavily** inside the suit ——————————

There are so many kernels

Lies clamped to the hull of the **incredible** alien city —————— *like a limpet*
a   special   area   has   been   carved   into   *that   section   of*   the   ship
like a borough in which the Greenmen have been invited to stay ***a refuge***
a habitat
an apology

ψ 1 F s ꟿ Ç 1 ≠ 0 1 г a 0 ∡ 1 g Æ 0 ꝧ 0 1 0 Đ 0 1 ¿ ¶ 0 А 0 1 £ ¤ 1 1 æ Ø 0 1 1 đ »
¥ § 1 ⇸ 0 Ç ^ ≼ *[We were experimenting with arcane science]* Ц Э ф л ⨎ Д 0
ꓵ ю Ж * Ф ¿ # *[Your temporal summoning was an accident]* Å a 1 Ø þ ā ¿ ±
¢ ~ ¡ Ç Д Ω ξ Ц Э ¡ *[Such research has since been halted]* ф л Д 0 ꓵ ю Ж Ф λ
Д А ± 0 ¢ ~ ¡ ¤ 1 ζ Θ Љ *[We cannot return you thence]* ? 0 ≢ ⅝ ₪ 1 ✳ Ȏ ħ й 1
¥ § 1 Љ Æ a § g f a ¿ # Å ζ *[But we can give you]* Ç Đ đ » ξ φ Ħ ꟿ ₪ Ç ^ 1 ¼ Ø
þ ā ¿ ✿ ¶ ψ Ħ « F ю Ж Ф λ ξ 1 φ *[community]* Ħ ₪ г Д f a ¿ # Å ζ a g Æ Ç Đ đ »
1 ? 1 Æ © Å æ Ø 1 Ç Д Ω ξ ◎ 1 ⊷ 1 Ҟ 0 ψ ₪ 1 ✳ Ȏ ħ й ∡ 1 g Æ 0 ꝧ Д 0 ꓵ ю Ф

So the Little Green Men *and women*
alone in the universe for so long *agreed*

forgave

accepted the offer *now live & thrive in*
⨎ ꟿ ю Д Ħ λ

↓ translated ↓

Future Traveller Town

The Д Ω ξ Ц Э φ *residents* agree it's where you can find the best pastrami

I have something for you!

Zroy says *excited* to her hand terminal

Janet follows the girl via screen—SecCamera—door sensor—HeatSig as she makes her way down to the Gamamemnon Invertebrator chamber

I dialed it up last night.

Janet knows

she's been haunting the mainframe

for the last week but has said nothing *because of all the human traits to endure over the millenia* feigning surprise at gifts has been unshakeable

They enter the chamber and see the shadowy mass in the final bioduct *the timer* ¡**ding!** patiently finishing its coalesce

Okay then, time to head in.

[Pardon the pun] Janet replies

as she *the program* slides on in

and then Janet **the person** slides right out

<u>SLOOOooOOOP!</u>

she lays there gasping amniofluid onto the floor

Zroy crouches next to her **proud as punch** and whispers sooths to the newborn

You're the very last one.

Spared no expense. Used Squink even; no kelp fibres in you, lady.

Made a couple tweaks here and there. Hope you like it.

She leans over *places a delicate kiss on Janet's brow*

pats the pile of fresh clothes on the floor beside her ***and leaves***

Vartalobelia stretches *languorous* across the bed ———————— rolls over to find the other side empty   pulls on *the bare minimum of* clothing and   makes   her   way   **blinking**   to   the   galley   for   the   ritual searing hot cup of revival liquid *then* **upship** *to the flight deck* and attempts to sneak up on Frij in the navigation seat

You do realise I have sensors for that sort of thing?

Pfft! No fun at all.

Flops into the pilot's seat **feet up on the dashboard** cradling her cup

Where we headed?

Thought I'd plot a course to see Minkowski's Butterfly.

Ooh! Romantic.

Then maybe on to Pohl's Kugelblitz?

Yeah—not so much.

a moment's quiet reflection while Frij clacks away at the NavConsole

she types like it's a martial art

What do the Elders think of you sightseeing around the cosmos?

I renegotiated my contract. I'm now sort of an...

...independent auditor. And debt collector.

And what happens when the Collective catch up to us?

Frij stops attacking the console ———] [——— exasperation turns to wonder and looks over at Varta —————] [————————— *turns to* desire

I took a new assignment this morning.

—Collecting a rogue asset for the Cob.

Varta's heart skips a beat & Frij **approaches** slowly *like a predator*

One day I'll catch you...

After such a long engagement a marriage *in any of its crazy forms*
can seem like a mere formality **and yet** it still contains a gloriousness
like the lustrous pearl within the ruffled
unkempt
discoloured shell *of familiarity*
there lies a magnificent hidden wonder

Lojol and Janet were discovering that wonder   *they're still on the farm*
and slowly **slowly** were *getting comfortable*   while their ship gets repaired
settling in —— relaxing —— restoring   ***another gift from the kingdom***

Janet's body had been a freebie but Lojol decided to stay and help with the
it was the least he could do   ...   clean-up
They snuggled   **a lot**
made love   explored
dinner parties   *with Zroy & Gunter*
you know   **grownup stuff**
One evening   *I need an offworlder with a bit of savvy.*   Zroy said
sound familiar?

What about the bounties on you, Honey?
It's all sorted, darlin'.
—————— Indeed it was ———— Janet may have been the last synth
to come out of the Invertebrator *but there were a couple extra Lojols before that*
Barely autonomous and distributed ***via Jezek*** to the offended parties
Oh Lojol   you   *Sneaky!*

The kelpfarm
commune
kingdom
is almost entirely in order again

field	by	net
node	*by*	*bubble*
room	by	closet

Gunter spies a **misplaced** object   an orb
handles either side

picks it up & —————————————————

i n a d v e r t a n t l y
s w i t c h i n g
the thing
on

—————————————————the machine takes all his thoughts—————————————
——— r e r o u t e s ——————— takes all his thoughts ——————— *ampl i f i e s* ———
——— *re connects* ——————— all his thoughts ——————— amp l e c t ī———
——— rev i s e s ————————— his thoughts ——————— *amp ersand* ———
————————————————— *THOUGHTeR!* —————————

Ach!
ERSTAUNLICH!

People; basically a lot of stuff with random connections
~ p. Grlgenheim

REF.ERE.NCE

And a special mention to **Federman**'s *'Double or Nothing'* & **Belgum**'s *'Star Fiction'*
without whose inspiration this book would never have been made